THE BEGGAR'S DREAM

VICTORIAN ROMANCE

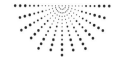

SADIE HOPE

JOIN MY NEWSLETTER

The Beggar's Dream

Sadie Hope was born in Preston, Lancashire, where she worked in a textile factory for many years. Married with two grown children, she would spend her nights writing stories about life in Victorian times. She loved to read all the books of this era and often found herself daydreaming of characters that would pop into her head.

She hopes you enjoy these stories for she has many more to share with you.

You can find Sadie on:

https://www.facebook.com/AuthorSadie Hope/

or

Join her newsletter http://eepurl.com/dOVZDb

THE BEGINNING

*I*t was a cold, rainy night in London. Abigail picked up the blackened old poker which leaned like a crooked old man against the small fireplace. Giving the burning embers a prod, she managed to get a bit more life going in the fire. Shuffling a little closer she wondered how long it would last as she tried to soak up the warmth as best she could.

If she closed her eyes, she could almost imagine she was relaxing inside her very own townhouse after a long but rewarding day at her shop. Her blonde hair would be pinned above her head in ringlets that curled around her face. The day had been spent sewing dresses for the most important ladies of

London. Perhaps Miles would be by her side, and they would hold hands in front of the fire, lazily enjoying their time together after a lavish meal.

The sound of her father's hacking cough brought her back to reality. Garth Patrick was sat on their only chair with his one leg propped up on an old crate that Abigail had found on the street. He was using it in place of a footstool.

"Are you okay, Father?" Abigail got to her feet and reached up to feel the temperature of his forehead. She brushed away the damp blond locks from his forehead and could see that his brown eyes were bloodshot. He had once told her that her blue eyes matched her mother's. How she wished that she was here now to turn to.

"Oh, I'm fine, my dear, nothing to worry about it," he croaked.

Despite his insistence, it was something to worry about indeed. His forehead was burning and he was sweating through his clothes, yet shivering at the same time. Abigail was in no doubt that it was a fever. She gave him a reproachful look before she moved back to the fire to tend to the pot of broth.

It contained the last of their food, every little scrap from the tiny kitchen at the back of their one-roomed home. Round and round she stirred, but the broth was getting no thicker. With a slight sigh she carefully poured it out into a bowl. Making sure not to spill a drop, she placed it on the table which was made from another crate with a rag placed over it, to try and make it look a little nicer. Her father tried to lean forward so that he could taste some but Abigail could see it took all of his strength to make the slight movement.

"No, Father, just you sit and relax, I'll help you," she said, gently pushing him back so that he was resting against the back of the chair. Slowly, she began to spoon the meager, watery broth into his mouth. With each spoonful she silently prayed that it would at least settle his hunger and allow him to get some of his strength back.

"I'm sorry, Abigail," he said sadly, "for not being able to give you the life you deserve."

Abigail opened her mouth to protest.

He waved a hand at her, cutting off the words that sat heavy in her throat. Then his sad eyes glanced around at their dismal surroundings. They had struggled for as long as Abigail could remember. They had been lucky to get these lodgings in East London. The small room being on the ground floor provided a huge relief to her father who had only the one leg. Their place was small and cramped and the rent was low, but it was still a struggle to get by.

"You know, things were different when your mother was still alive." He leaned his head back in the chair, having finished supping the last of the broth and launched into a story with a faraway look in his eyes and a glimmer of a smile.

"We were young and very much in love. I'll never forget the first time we met. I was dressed in my red uniform, all new and freshly pressed, proudly riding my horse on my way to battle. Your mother was feeding an apple to her own horse over the fence and stroking its nose as I rode by. I called out "are you lost, m'lady?" with a cheeky grin. "She whirled around, her hands on her hips and put me in my place: '*I should think not. You're the stranger around here.*'"

A sigh escaped him and she thought she saw the shine of tears in his eyes.

"In an instant I was smitten, she was a right beauty and with a bit of spark in her too. I apologised, playing humble, and got down from my horse to introduce myself properly. Oh, I can't tell you how she made me feel. Maybe it was going to war but I think she was just special... your mother. I rode away promising to write to her and sure as anything I kept my word. Her letters kept me going during the tough times of war. Giving me hope and something to fight for. I arrived home victorious and we were soon married."

A cough stopped the story for a few moments but Abigail was spellbound and wanted to hear more. "Tell me all about it," she said when the cough subsided.

"Well, sadly, Wendy's family weren't happy about the match, I can tell you. The Dunkley family were gentry you see and your mother was supposed to be married off to a Lord, not a poor soldier. We were too in love to care about what they thought so we eloped and they all but cut her off for it.

"After a while, her parents' disapproval weighed heavy on Wendy and she spoke to them. Eventually, Mrs Dunkley could see that Wendy was happy and that I would do anything for her daughter. They didn't welcome me into the family with open arms but agreed to provide some of Wendy's inheritance so that she could have some semblance of a life fitting for a lady.

"We got set up in a beautiful cottage in the countryside. Pretty flowers decorated the garden, we had fields and a stable for horses and your mother made the whole place a home. And just in time too, for you came along shortly after.

"The spitting image of your mother you were, we were a happy family for those first five years, until duty called and I was sent away to war once more. Wendy hated it when I had to leave but I was filled with pride and determination to defend my country for my two girls at home. Even so, I ached to be away from you both. It felt like all my wildest dreams had come true." He paused for a moment, deep in thought before his indulgent smile faded slightly, turning into longing and sadness.

"But during one battle I was... struck down, losing my leg and was sent home for good, no longer able to fulfil my duties as a soldier. With some difficulty we got by, Wendy having occasional help from her parents and I eventually managed to secure a bit of work keeping accounts at the local shop.

"Everything looked like it was going to be okay until that terrible day when your mother died in a horse-riding accident. The Dunkleys cut us off completely, raising the rent on the cottage so that we were forced to move. Crippled and carrying what little belongings I could, I took us into the city and found us room and board in a crumbling old Inn. It took me weeks to secure the job with Mr Walter and by that point all our savings were nearly gone."

Abigail didn't need to hear the rest, she knew how the story went, her hollow stomach rumbled loudly as if to remind her. It had been nice to know more about her mother, though. She'd never heard her father speak about the life they used to have before. His words interrupted her thoughts and she turned back to him. Then she could see that it was the light of love that lit his eyes and she prayed that one day she too would feel that light.

"You look more and more like your mother every day," her father said fondly.

Abigail smiled, filled with pride. There was a picture

of her mother with her father and Abigail as a baby above the fireplace. Her mother had been very beautiful and her father was lit up with more joy than she'd ever seen on his face. They looked like something out of a fairy tale, so far removed from the life Abigail knew now.

A loud cough interrupted Abigail from her thoughts.

"I think it's time for my medicine," her father wheezed. He was often in poor health, blaming the damp walls, the smoky air and the diseased rats which populated the city.

Abigail jumped up from her spot on the floor in front of the fire and fetched the bottle of medicine from the shelf. With great care, she measured out the foul-smelling liquid into a cup and held it out to her father.

"Thanks, Abigail," he said, pushing himself up with a groan and taking the cup from her with a shaking hand. He gulped it back in one go, his face screwed up in disgust, "It's lovely stuff."

She laughed, relieved that he still had a sense of humour.

"I think that's bedtime, Abi," he said pointedly.

She wasn't sleepy but there was little point trying to stay up with an empty stomach.

She picked up his walking sticks and held them out so that he could get up out of the chair. As he pulled himself up to hop across the small room Abigail was relieved to see that there was a bit of colour in his previously white cheeks. Though, he was a long way off looking healthy, with his bony frame, and the permanent shadows under his eyes.

"I can take the floor this time," he offered but his insistence was half-hearted and she shook her head.

"No, Father, you need your rest or all that medicine will go to waste." She knew how hard he worked, but he got little in return and he was always complaining about how expensive the medicine was.

After he got into their only bed, he said goodnight and closed his eyes. Abigail moved quietly back to the front of the fireplace. The fire was simmering down but it was still nice and warm so she got as cosy as she could with the ragged grey blanket. She was used to the floor though at times she dreamed of feather beds and cotton sheets. These were things she would have one day, but more importantly she would have food.

As she closed her eyes, she daydreamed wistfully about the life her father had narrated, imagining how different things might be if her mother was still alive. It was so far removed from their real lives. One where they had no food to wake up to, her father was sick with a fever and she was all he had.

Tomorrow would be better, she told herself, she would get work in the shop, have enough pennies to bring something home for dinner and they'd make it to the end of the day without rumbling bellies and the enduring ache of despair that came with constant hunger.

Just a few more years working in the dress shop and she'd be qualified to be a top seamstress. Then, when she was old enough, she'd be able to inherit the shop and be in charge of designing the really expensive pretty dresses that the rich ladies wore. She was always in awe of the fitted, flowing gowns she saw them wearing, imagining that one day she could look like a princess too and then she'd sweep Miles off his feet just like her mum did with her father.

Closing her eyes and rolling over, she wriggled around until she was comfortable enough, listening to the soft snoring of her father and the rumbling of her empty stomach. She wished that her daydreams would all come true, that she could have a nice warm bed to sleep in and enough food so that they never went hungry.

Eventually, the shouts from the streets outside and the stomping of footsteps upstairs faded out as Abigail drifted off into sleep. Her dreams were filled with her mother's smiling face. Then her mother was walking away. Each time she turned a corner she was wearing a different dress. They were all so beautiful, embroidered with ribbon. Abigail kept running through the dirt-laden streets but she could never catch up. Panting and with tears running down her face she caught a glance of her own reflection in the window of the grocer. Her face dirty with soot and her stained white dress looking like a ragged old sack.

Her shabby reflection was replaced with the sight of a loaf of bread, displayed proudly in the window. It looked so tasty and she could smell the freshly baked scent wafting out through the open door. It made her mouth water and her stomach growl with desperation. Her hand reached out to grab it but the Baker yelled out and shook his broomstick at her.

"Get out of here, you dirty vagrant."

The words echoed in her mind and she had to sniff back her tears. Soon all was quiet, her father's snores easing into deep breathing as he rolled over onto his side. Abigail curled up in a ball and basked in the subtle glow as the fire finally faded out, leading the way to a soothing dreamless sleep.

2

THE DECISION

*A*bigail awoke the next morning to the sight of her father already awake bright and early.

"Morning, Abigail," he called out from the other side of the room.

"Good morning," she yawned, stiff from sleeping on the floor all night.

"Give me a hand carrying the pot, would you?" He was holding a pot of water, nodding his head toward the fire. Seeing him up and about was a good sign. The pale pallor was gone from his face but she could see his arms shaking as he held the water.

Clambering to her feet, she rubbed the sleep from her eyes and hurried across the room to take the pot from his hands, placing it above the fire to boil. He must have tended to the fire while she was still sleeping for it was burning steadily rather than fading to nothing more than a flicker like she'd expected.

"How are you feeling?" she asked, picking up the two chipped cups for the tea.

"Oh, a bit better," he said before his cough started.

Though he looked better Abigail really didn't like the sound of his cough. It was deep and liquid and sometimes it made her think of drowning.

Soon the water was boiling and Abigail poured out two cups of tea. It had been a while since they'd been able to afford sugar so they'd grown used to having it black and unsweetened. While her father was looking a bit better, the fever hadn't completely left. He needed a real meal, some meat to replenish his strength.

In a flash, she dressed and got ready to head for the dress shop where she sometimes worked. It would all be okay. She'd get work for the day and have enough money to buy meat to bring home. They would survive another day, just like they'd always done.

The clouds lay heavy in the sky as Abigail stepped out into the street. She prayed internally for the rain to hold off, looking down at her worn shoes and threadbare coat. It was a long walk to the shop. Despite her wish, the sky opened and it began to gush down with rain.

Darting through the streets of London she did her best to stay dry. Her journey took her through the dark sooty slums to pass by the nice houses. All the time she kept her head down to try and avoid getting wet. It did little good though, by the time she reached the shop she was soaked through from head to toe, the thought of the warm fire inside was the only thing keeping her going.

Running across the road, her eyes on the door, she didn't even notice the oncoming carriage until the driver yelled at her to get out of the way.

"Oi! Watch where you're going!"

Just in time she looked up to swerve out of the way of the horses, listening to the man curse her as they rode past. Her heart hammering from the shock, she wrapped her arms across her front and stepped onto the pavement, taking a few shaky steps to the shop door before entering.

It was early but Mrs Hardcastle's Haberdashery was already open. The owner was stitching a garment behind the counter. To look at, she was an elegant woman who always took pride in her appearance, yet she had a hard tongue on her and settled for no-nonsense. Her dark hair was pinned into a neat bun, with a few hints of grey around the edges.

She peered up over her glasses as Abigail entered the shop, flicking her eyes back to her work as she spoke.

"Don't you be traipsing in all that water on my floor!" she called out.

"Sorry, Mrs Hardcastle," Abigail said, making a move towards the fire to try and dry off a bit.

"I ain't got no work for you so there's no point staying."

Abigail's heart sank at these words, she desperately needed the work.

"Surely there's something I can help you with? Anything at all and I'll do it, please." She tried to keep her voice steady but her emotions betrayed her, the wobble in her voice as plain as day.

Before Mrs Hardcastle could answer, the little bell above the door rang to announce a customer coming in. Mrs Hardcastle turned her attention to the lady and greeted her politely, quickly striking up a conversation.

Panic coursed through Abigail. Perhaps she could approach the lady herself, offer her services at half the price, with home deliveries, anything she wanted. For a moment she almost called out but trying to take business from right under Mrs Hardcastle's nose would cost her a job and she'd never get work in the shop again.

Still, she hovered at the side of the room, praying that Mrs Hardcastle would require her help for whatever this lady wanted; surely, there would be more work now.

"I'm not running an open house here," Mrs Hardcastle screamed after the customer had left. "I said there was no work so scram, will you!"

Her face burning, Abigail all but ran out of the door, her shoulders hunched and eyes pricking with tears.

She hurried out of sight of the shop, blinking furiously and willing herself not to cry. *It's okay, I'll find work elsewhere. It'll be okay, it will.*

As much as she tried to give herself a pep talk, panic took hold, coursing through her like poison. Eyes burning, she felt tears begin to stream down her cheeks. She felt like nothing more than a common street urchin after being turned away by Mrs Hardcastle. Stumbling out onto a busy street, she wiped her eyes, drying them as best she could with her damp sleeve.

The rain had stopped and a spot of sun was drying it out. It was like a burst of hope giving her a new leap of confidence. She may be begging today but she had a dream and things would get better.

She approached a passer-by in the street, trying to arrange her face into a look of wide-eyed innocence. "Can you spare any change, Sir?"

"Get away from me, you dirty varmint."

It felt like hours went by. Abigail endured nothing but sneers, cold eyes looking over the top of her head, and rich people muttering to each other about the disgrace of beggars and how they should be locked up in the poor house. One woman even kicked her out into the road after she'd continued to plead with the well-dressed stranger.

It was so unfair. People like that had everything they could ever want and more; money, a big house with servants to wait on them, the women would be married to a well-to-do husband... and Abigail had nothing but her father, who struggled to take care of himself, let alone her. These people didn't need the money but they couldn't even part with a couple of pennies to help her.

The aching rumble in her stomach propelled her forward and she glanced at the row of shops coming up. Surely, at least one of them would have work going.

"I'll have no beggars in here, girl!" the red-faced matron in the tailor's yelled at her as soon as she entered the dress shop, waving a broom at her.

"But I just-"

"I said no beggars in my shop!"

"No, no, I'm not a beggar, I'm a seamstress, Madam, I just-" She couldn't get a sentence out however without being shut down by the angry outbursts of the large woman.

The next couple of shops were less hostile but all of the shopkeepers venomously shook their heads in answer to Abigail's query about any work for the day. Losing all hope, she roamed the streets aimlessly, not being able to stomach any more rejections or dirty looks.

"Miss Abigail, how nice to see you." A vaguely familiar voice sounded out and she looked up to see the oily smirk of Mr Samuel. He was well-known in certain circles, running a gang of pickpockets around the city.

"Oh, hello, Mr Samuel," she greeted him politely. The many stories she'd heard about him and his men were both impressive and terrifying.

"You look rather worse for wear my dear if you don't mind me saying." He looked down his long nose at her, his smile bordering between polite and something predatory, setting off a lurch of fear in the pit of her stomach.

"Oh, well, I...."

"I rather think there's something I could do to help with that," he interrupted her stuttering before she could think of anything to say. "I could use a nice girl like you. With the right clothes and attitude nobody would suspect a thing."

Join Mr Samuel's gang?

She caught her breath, feeling herself almost giving in to the temptation. He was the master at thievery and could teach her everything she needed in order to make a good living picking pockets. There would be no more hungry nights, no more begging for work. Maybe her father would be well if he got some good food in his belly?

"I run a tight ship but my guys are well looked after. I can teach you everything you need to know, you could be my crowning jewel," he said.

"Oi, Oi, Boss," an unfamiliar voice called out.

Abigail turned to see an older boy approach. He was tall and skinny with a pair of dark eyes that bored into her like he was seeing right through her.

"Zackery," Mr Samuel nodded, "what have you got for me?"

Zackery pulled a bag of coins from his pocket, a smug smirk on his face as he looked at Abigail again. Mr Samuel grabbed it from him, took a quick look through the bag before taking a cut of the coins and tossing the rest back to the pickpocket.

"Now, scram!" Mr Samuel said, waving off the boy whose gaze was fixated on Abigail, making her feel slightly sick.

"What do you say, Abigail?" he tilted his head to the side, his eyes boring into hers in that horrid uncomfortable way, like he had a hidden plan for her. She shivered, feeling sick to the pit of her stomach.

How can I consider such a thing? Father has always taught me that stealing is wrong, that dishonesty is a sin. There will be more work soon, and I'll be able to make it as a top seamstress eventually.

"No, thank you, Mr Samuel, I'm quite all right." Her voice quivered slightly as she gave her answer, hoping he'd disappear soon and she could be rid of his foreboding presence.

"Well, if you change your mind..." he winked before turning on his heel and being on his way, seeming completely unruffled at Abigail turning down his offer.

A shiver ran through her as she turned to walk in the opposite direction. Despite it being the long way home, she wanted to leave behind any trace of him and her brief moment considering herself as a thief both protected and imprisoned in his pocket.

3

UNWANTED ATTENTIONS

With Mr Samuel well behind her, Abigail headed towards Walter's Greengrocer, rubbing together the few coins that remained in her pocket. Her stomach fluttered as she thought of Miles, her best friend, hoping he'd be there when she arrived as he often was.

She was looking forward to the chance to talk and joke with him, to forget her troubles for a moment. During one of their walks exploring the streets of London they each shared their dreams for the future. At nearly fifteen-years-old she wondered if she was too old to be daydreaming, but it was all she had and that future called to her. If she kept it in her mind then one day it would come true, she just knew it.

Then she remembered Miles and his dreams and how proud she was of him.

"Mine is to be a solicitor, to learn the law and fight for justice," he'd said. "I told my father but he did nothing but laugh. '*Professions like that are for over-educated brats swimming in riches,* he said. *You're to grow up and take over the shop when I retire, keeping it in the family.*'"

He'd sounded so disappointed when he shared his father's reaction with her. She told him all about her own ambition to be a top seamstress and run her own shop one day. They strolled along the river, animatedly imagining how their lives would look in the future, her heart fluttering when he talked of them having fancy dinners together and enjoying the spoils of the city.

It wasn't difficult to fall for Miles and his kind blue eyes and perfect blonde hair. Not only that, he was a good person and a loyal friend but she knew that she would never be a good enough match for someone like him.

If Miles was there, then she had a good chance of getting some scraps of meat and a bit of work for the afternoon. As long as Mr Walter wasn't around. He didn't believe in charity, compassion or anything humane as far as Abigail could tell. Her father worked for him as an accountant and he expected his employees to work hard for a scraping of coin, even if they were on their death beds.

She longed to buy a chicken and some vegetables to make a good hearty soup. There was nothing like it to soothe a fever and chase away illness, it would be just what her father needed and also would help to fill up her empty belly. But she knew that she didn't have enough money for meat like that, the longing for Miles to be working increasing as she thought about her situation.

As the bell rang to announce the door opening, Abigail stepped into Walter's Greengrocer and felt her heart sink. Miles was nowhere to be seen, for it was Jerome Walter who stood there manning the counter, his greedy piggy eyes falling on her as soon as she was in the door.

"Good afternoon, Miss..." he called out, his eyes raking over her, pausing to lick his lips appreciatively.

"Good afternoon, Mr Walter," she said politely, trying to fix a smile onto her face despite the bubbling discomfort she felt at the way he was looking at her.

Dropping her eyes, she busied herself by examining the goods on display, pretending to consider the meat despite knowing that the measly coins she held in her fist couldn't cover the cost. All she could afford was a little bit of flour. Her best hope was to forage for some mushrooms and eggs.

Jerome's eyes trailed after her every movement like a lion stalking his prey. Her discomfort growing, she weighed out a portion of grain and a couple of handfuls of flour and hastily shoved her coins on the counter.

Before she could snatch her hand out of reach, he grabbed hold of it, squeezing tight so that she couldn't wriggle out of his grasp. At last he loosened his fist and trailed his fingers across her palm before picking up the coins from the counter.

Abigail's heart pounded against her chest and she fought the urge to vomit. There was nothing in her stomach but still, she didn't wish to lose anything.

"I hope to see your father at work tomorrow morning, I've quite the stack of paperwork building up," he all but growled.

"I'm sure you can rely upon him, Sir," Abigail squeaked, feeling uncomfortable being under his scrutiny with no-one else there. She snatched her hand away and he looked at her for a long few moments, saying not a word. Eventually she reached out to pick up her groceries and wished him a good day, trying not to openly cringe as she felt his gaze follow her out of the shop door.

4

MUSHROOMS AND MEAT

*A*bigail let out a long breath as she stepped outside, closing the door behind her. *Thank goodness I got out of there.* Wrapping her arms around her waist, she started to hurry away but a familiar voice called out, causing her heart to flutter and pausing her in her tracks.

"Abigail!"

She whirled around and came face to face with Miles, waving with a sunny grin on his face.

"Miles! Hi." She couldn't help but smile at the sight of him, it was such a relief to see him after that awful encounter with his father. Sometimes, it was hard to believe that they were related, the two of them were so different. Where Jerome was bitter and twisted, Miles was sweetness and light.

"I've just been out doing deliveries for my father," he said. "This shop keeping malarkey never ends. Where are you off to?"

Without shame or worry she told him of her father's illness and how she was unable to get work for the day. "I'm heading out to search for mushrooms and eggs, things I won't have to buy."

"Let me come with you, we can make an afternoon of it," Miles announced. "We can be a team of hunters scouring the city, returning home to feed our adoring families with our bountiful find."

Abigail laughed, taking his waiting arm. He always found a way to turn the worst situation around, injecting fun and laughter into it until it felt like nothing but a game between friends.

"Onwards!" he announced.

Abigail noticed that he wheeled her around so that they were well out of sight of his father's shop. Not that she was complaining.

"I take it you don't have permission for this little adventure?" Abigail teased.

"Well... not exactly. I'm supposed to be picking something up for my father but if he asks, Mrs Crockett wasn't at the market today."

"If he quizzes me, I'll say just that," she said, smiling at him.

"How's your father coping?" Miles asked, his tone turning more serious.

"He's..." Abigail sighed as she launched in, "he's been quite unwell. Taking care of him has been difficult at times." She told him all about the infection, resulting in a fever which had been plaguing him for some time now. How he'd been unable to work, and even that they were on the verge of starving.

"Sometimes I wonder how we'll be able to keep surviving like this," there was an audible wobble in her voice as she felt herself well up. She had to stay strong at home, to encourage her father's recovery, keeping his spirits up, but with Miles she could open up and tell him her deepest fears and her darkest worries.

They'd slowed their pace right down and Miles tugged gently on her hand to pull her to a stop, putting his arms around her. As they hugged, she felt protected in his arms, like everything was going to be okay. If only she could stay safe like this forever.

"Come on, let's get those mushrooms. I know of a place they grow so freely you'll have enough for a feast!" he tugged on her hand and they went running through the quieter streets, giggling like they were still young children.

Miles indeed lived up to his promise, helping her to collect as many mushrooms as they could carry. They even managed to spot a pigeon's nest. Miles climbed up the magnificent oak tree, shimmying out along a limb above the nest. It was precarious and his weight bent the bough down so that he could reach the eggs below.

"It's filled with decent sized eggs," he called, carefully placing them in his pockets for the climb down.

With a huge smile on her face Abagail carefully wrapped them up in leaves to stop them from getting broken on the walk home. By the time they arrived at her front door she was worn out from all the walking but she felt like all the disappointment from this morning was far behind her.

She was a little nervous explaining to her father that she'd not been able to get work, and that there was no money for meat, producing the eggs and mushrooms which now felt rather measly in comparison.

"Oh, that will do nicely, Abigail, I'm sure there will be plenty of work again. Tomorrow is a new day."

There was no disappointment in his voice, to her relief, and she set about making the tea and tidying up their sparse living space. It was no fancy townhouse. The East London slums were filled with beggars, starving families and all sorts of unsavoury people. No matter how hard she tried, there was always a lingering smell of damp and sewage from the streets outside and the unkempt building they lived in.

This was no reason not to make the best of what they had however. It may be small and squalid but it was the only home they had. By the time she'd scrubbed the sheets and blankets clean, hanging them out the window to dry, swept the floor and washed up, she was more than ready for dinner.

Chopping the onion and mushrooms she placed them in a pan to simmer. Her father woke up from his rest as the smell of cooking reached his nostrils.

"Ah, just in time," he croaked before a cough erupted from his chest.

Abigail glanced at him, frowning with worry. He had seemed so much better this morning, but without a decent meal how was he ever going to recover? Trying not to think about it, she turned her attention back to the pan, praying that the eggs would do for tonight. She supposed they were better than nothing.

An unexpected knock at the door made her jump, drawing her attention away from the cooking. She frowned at her father to see his eyebrows furrowed, a look of worry etched into his face. It aged him in an instant.

"Who is it?" he yelled out.

"It's Miles Walter, Mr Patrick."

Abigail brightened immediately at the sound of his voice and she all but skipped to fling the door open.

"Miles!" She exclaimed at the sight of him, opening the door wide to let him in. She felt slightly embarrassed at the prospect of Miles seeing where she lived, it was hardly a neighbourhood fit for a Merchant's son but she was relieved that she'd cleaned the place up so at least their small living space was looking as good as it ever would.

"Good evening, Miles, to what do we owe the pleasure?" her father asked, reaching for his stick to stand up and greet their guest.

"Good evening, Mr Patrick, Abigail," Miles said seamlessly nodding at them both. "There was a bit of ham going spare that simply won't keep another day. My father already has plenty of meat to feed us for a week and I thought perhaps I'd stop by and see if you'd like to take it off my hands? I'd hate to see a good bit of ham go to waste."

"Why, that's awfully kind of you, lad." Mr Patrick broke into a smile and hopped forward to shake Miles's spare hand. "I'm sure Abigail and I would be happy to oblige."

Abigail could have kissed Miles for this. Father wouldn't have taken kindly to pity, especially from the son of his employer. The way Miles spun it, as if they were doing him a favour by taking the ham, was incredibly thoughtful, he always knew just what to say.

As she took the ham, she whispered her thanks.

"Why don't you join us for dinner?" her father asked.

"That's awful nice of you to ask, Sir, but I'm afraid I'm needed back at the shop." Miles flashed his eyes at Abigail and a look of understanding passed between them. He knew how badly they needed the meat and it was highly unlikely that his uncharitable father, Jerome Walter, would willingly give away a chunk of ham.

She smiled back at him, her eyes filled with gratitude before he wished them both goodnight and headed on home.

There was nothing like a nourishing meal to soothe the soul. For the first night in ages, Abigail shared a laugh with her father, her full belly spreading a wave of relaxation through her whole body. She felt doubly happy at the sight of some real colour in her father's face. Going to bed full of optimism she fell into an easy, restful sleep.

5

DREAMS AND DREAD

*T*he cold, damp winter months finally gave way to the fresh lightness of spring and Abigail began to feel like she could breathe again. As the dark evenings lifted, so did her father's illness. It had been a long, difficult couple of months. Most of his earnings from Jerome went towards paying for medicine and the little he had after that paid the rent. She sometimes got work in Mrs Hardcastle's shop and when she didn't, she managed to scrounge some coins by begging. Occasionally, someone would take pity on her and depart with some good coins but more often than not she came home with nothing more than a couple of pennies.

The spring months passed and she fell into an easy

routine of work, begging and scraping food together. She was getting good at making meals out of what they had, trying to remain positive.

Soon enough Abigail felt her spirits rise as summer arrived. It was her absolute favourite season. People always looked happier and lighter without the need to wrap up from the bitter chill of winter.

Mrs Hardcastle always referred to it as her busy season, lots of ladies requiring new party frocks, or summer dresses for being seen out about town.

"Fashions are always changing," she would say, "nobody wants to be seen out in society in the same gowns as last year."

This was good news for Abigail as it meant steady work. All the more chance to practice her seamstress skills.

Abigail worked hard throughout spring on the days that she'd been able to get work and it seemed to be paying off for Mrs Hardcastle was becoming more appreciative of her. It was like that terrible day in the rain where she'd sent her packing because she had no work had never happened.

"Now, girl, have you finished that hemline yet?" Mrs Hardcastle called through one day.

"Yes, Mrs Hardcastle, I'm just checking over it now," she'd replied. Abigail was particularly proud of having double stitched the hemline of this dress and she had done a wonderful job. It was made out of such delicate and fine material. Mrs Hardcastle had impressed upon her how important it was to take her time with it and not to tear the fabric.

As she carried the finished dress through to the front, the woman's sharp eyes scanned every inch of the garment like an eagle evaluating its prey. At the end, Abigail earned a satisfactory nod and an appreciative raising of the eyebrows. After this, Mrs Hardcastle began to refer to her as Miss Patrick instead of 'girl' or 'you there.'

Life was good, even her friendship with Miles was blossoming and they began to spend more and more time together.

"I swear you've gotten taller in the past couple of weeks!" Abigail exclaimed as they went on one of their regular strolls alongside the river.

"Perhaps I'm becoming a grown up before my time,"

Miles joked as Abigail tried to measure herself against him. He made light of it but the childish roundness was all but gone from his face and his arms and chest were broad and appeared strong. She felt like a silly little girl in comparison.

"Don't worry, I won't become too old and boring to hang out with you," he said lightly.

"You'd better not, otherwise I'd have to find some new friends."

"Well, I don't think you'd have any trouble there," he said pointedly, his eyes fixed to her left.

She turned around to see what he was looking at. Zachery, the boy from Mr Samuel's gang of pickpockets was slowly walking a few paces behind them. Abigail rolled her eyes and turned back to Miles. "Please. He's a pickpocket, he's probably sizing you up as a mark," she said quietly so that Zachery wouldn't hear her.

"I don't think it's me he's looking at," Miles countered, "and this isn't the first time I've seen him tailing us." He grabbed Abigail's hand and pulled her sharply to the right in the direction of the market. "Come on."

They ducked and dived through the crowds of people and market stalls which sported a variety of different wares until they were well clear of Zachery.

"So, come on now, imagine you've just closed up your shop for the day and I'm taking you out to buy you a present. What would you choose?"

They fell into their favourite game; pretending that she ran her very own shop as a seamstress and that Miles worked as a successful solicitor. They had plenty of money for food and riches, could afford to pay for her father's care and Miles was making enough to get him as far away from his father as possible.

"Why, these necklaces are simply lovely," Abigail spoke in her posh lady voice.

"These are the latest fashion, or so I'm told," Miles played along. "This one would certainly bring out your eyes." He pointed to a silver chain which held a simple blue stone in the centre which matched the colour of her eyes.

"Why, you have such a good eye, Mr Walter," Abigail said as she curtseyed, trying to suppress a giggle.

"You bring it out in me." He bowed in return, a grin forming on his face.

The market vendor looked at the pair of them suspiciously, dragging his eyes over Abigail's simple cotton dress and worn shoes.

"Let's go, Miss Patrick, there's plenty more to explore before we find the perfect piece." Miles made a show of drawling over his words, putting on the most snobbish voice he could muster.

As they strode off arm in arm, they heard an almighty, "Harrumph" from the grumpy vendor and they burst into a fit of giggles as soon as they were out of his sight.

"How are things with your father?" Abigail asked. She knew that there was a lot of tension between the two of them, that Miles didn't want to follow in his father's footsteps and live in his shadow in the shop.

Miles sighed, kicking the stones on the ground as they strolled down one of the paths, his hands in his pockets.

"They're the same as ever. He caught me reading a

book on current legislation the other day and you know what he did? He knocked it right out of my hand and said 'what the hell are you doing with that? I told you to give up this solicitor nonsense, your future is nothing but the four walls of my darned shop!'"

"Oh, Miles, that's awful." Her heart went out to him, he was so smart and determined, she wished she could do something to help.

"My Auntie Pat believes in me, you know. She's the only family I have besides my father." He went on to tell her that she'd always encouraged him, giving him advice, buying him books and helping him to find good hiding places for them so that Jerome couldn't see them and retaliate.

"I wish I could live with her instead of my father," he said wistfully.

"Perhaps things will get better and your father will start to see that the shop is not for you, that you're too smart to waste it all in that place," Abigail said, looping her arm through his.

"Perhaps," he said, unconvincingly, before changing the subject, discussing the different market stalls and speculating how much money the stall merchants might earn.

They explored the market a bit more; Abigail was drawn to a table of fabrics while Miles checked out the selection of meats on offer, scouring for a bargain. As she ran her fingers carefully over a pretty pale pink sample of silk, she heard an unfamiliar voice speak her name behind her.

"Hi, Abigail."

She whirled around to find the pickpocket, Zachery, towering over her, a look of satisfaction on his face as if he was pleased to have finally got her alone.

"See anything you like?" He eyed the wares suggestively.

"What are you doing here?" she demanded.

"Looking for something I like the look of." His tone made her skin crawl as his gaze travelled slowly over her and she took a step back instinctively.

"I don't know you. Stop following me," she insisted.

"Well, I know you. Abigail Patrick. My boss thinks you'd be quite the addition to our little family."

Family? Oh please. You're nothing more than a common street gang of thieves. Abigail felt an uncomfortable wriggle of relief as she remembered her brief moment in considering asking Mr Samuel to take her on. How glad she was that she saw sense and decided against it.

"No, thank you," Abigail said coolly, fixing her gaze back to the pink fabric she was examining before Zachery had turned up. Keeping her back to him she was willing for him to go away and leave her alone. *Don't you have innocent people's pockets to empty?* She wanted to ask but the last thing she wished to do was encourage him.

"You don't know what you're missing," he goaded, taking a step closer to her.

"Please, just leave me alone," she exclaimed.

"I know you don't mean that," he breathed, his eyes looking her up and down.

"She said to leave her alone," Miles's voice sounded out, offering a threat in its tone as he appeared behind Zackery. "You'd better get lost before I do something I regret," he continued as he stepped in close beside Abigail

Miles slid his arm around her shoulders in a protective gesture, looking down at Zachery with cold eyes and his lips in a straight line. She'd never seen him look this angry before.

It did the trick, for Zachery snorted before shrugging his hands in his pockets and slouching away from them, Abigail sighing in relief at the sight of him finally walking away.

"Thank you, Miles," she said, leaning in against him slightly, feeling cosy and safe with his arm wrapped around her.

"It's no problem. Let me know if he bothers you again. You don't want to be getting mixed up with the likes of him."

Miles gave her shoulder a squeeze before moving his arm away again, much to her dismay. Abigail felt a prickle of shame, keeping quiet about how close she'd once come to doing just that.

6

A SAD GOODBYE

"*A*bigail, I need that gown to be packed up and ready in 5!" Mrs Hardcastle barked from the front of the shop. It was another warm summer morning which had Abigail up and out at the crack of dawn to get to work.

"Coming right up!" Abigail called back. She'd already finished stitching the seam and was in the process of carefully folding the light summer gown to wrap it in paper ready for Miss Pierce to collect it. It was one of her favourite dresses. A light cream colour falling effortlessly to the ground with simple black stitching around the collar and neckline, matching ribbons flowing around the short sleeves and corset area.

With a practiced hand, she quickly wrapped up the dress after making sure every inch of it was perfect, hurrying through the beaded curtain to the front of the shop she placed it on the counter.

"Right, I'm going to need you to get started on the order from Miss Carr, it's been non-stop out here." Mrs Hardcastle's usually neat hair was unravelling at the sides but that was the only hint of pressure; other than that, she was her usual orderly and no-nonsense self.

"Yes, Mrs Hardcastle." Abigail dashed back through as Miss Pierce entered the shop to collect her dress, a feeling of excitement shooting through her. She'd been hoping for a chance to work on some of the more elaborate dresses and this one certainly fit the bill. Digging out the pattern, she examined it until she was familiar with the cut, shape and fabric required, heading into the storeroom to find everything she needed.

Abigail had lost count of how many dresses she'd stitched, jackets she'd repaired, hems she'd fixed... it had been a very busy summer and it was showing no signs of slowing down. Her fingers constantly ached from holding a needle, her upper back was aching with stiffness after spending so much time hunched over her work.

Despite all that, Abigail was happy. She was getting much faster at sewing and had developed a keen eye for detail and fashion. Learning so much she was well on her way to becoming a top seamstress. She still had a way to go before she would be good enough to earn a full-time place in Mrs Hardcastle's Haberdashery but hopefully by the same time next summer arrived she'd be there.

The long days in the shop provided her with enough money to have a constant supply of food. Even though it would soon be winter again, Abigail wasn't worried. She'd even managed to stock up on some extra coal so that they'd be prepared.

After finishing up another long day in the dress shop, she wearily made her way to the Walters' grocery to pick up some ingredients for dinner. It was conveniently located on her way home from Mrs Hardcastle's. Tonight, she was thinking a nice hearty stew would do the trick. Also, she was hoping to see Miles. When she stepped in through the door her heart sank at the sight of Jerome, fixating his piggy eyes on her as soon as she walked in.

Her nose filled with all the usual smells inside the shop. The freshly baked bread, the sharp herby scents and the fleshly essence of the uncooked meat on display. Miles was nowhere to be seen so she quickly looked out a bit of beef and took it to the counter to pay, her stomach churning in discomfort at having to interact with Jerome.

"Nice to see you, Abigail," he purred in that foreboding way he had.

"Good evening, Mr Walter," she said tightly "Is my father here?"

"He's in the back finishing up the paperwork. He tells me that you are working with a Mrs Hardcastle as a seamstress?" Jerome asked rather piercingly.

"Yes, I am indeed," she responded, unsure why he was taking a sudden interest in her life.

"That must be hard work for a girl your age," he commented smoothly, like there was a hidden agenda underneath his words.

"Well, it's very busy at the moment but I enjoy the work," she stated as plainly as she could.

He considered her for a moment before responding,

"I suppose you can go and see if your father has finished his work for the day."

"Thank you, Mr Walter." Something about his tone made her sense he was up to something but she couldn't begin to guess what it was.

"Follow me," he ordered, producing a heavy set of jangling keys from his pocket, unlocking the door around the back of the shop.

All Abigail could see was darkness as he led her down a narrow hallway. Shivering with discomfort, she wrapped her arms around her middle and held on tightly as she took a tentative step after him.

Soon he was rattling on another door.

"Garth, you done in there?" he yelled out, "your daughter is here to pick you up," he practically spat out the words.

She listened to the shuffling sound as her father moved across the room to open the door.

"Ah, Mr Walter, hello, Abigail," her father greeted them.

"Have you finished those accounts?" Jerome barked.

Abigail could see a towering stack of papers on the desk.

"Almost, Sir," her father responded, a slight nervous twitch to his voice.

"Well, I need them finished tonight. And at what point did I say that you were allowed to have your family members traipsing in whenever the fancy takes them?" Jerome didn't even wait for an answer before slamming the door shut and turning to smirk at Abigail.

Silently, she hurried back to the front of the shop, Jerome hot on her heels. *You did that on purpose,* she thought, *just to humiliate my father and make me see that you have control over our family.* She couldn't stand the man. How could Miles be so nice and full of life with a father as wretched as this?

Jerome soon turned his attention to a waiting customer and Abigail flitted in relief from his sight, cheering up at the sight of Miles by the door and, as always, she felt her heart flutter as he smiled at her.

"Abigail! You're here," he exclaimed, "I feel like I've barely seen you for days."

"Miles!" an infectious smile spread through her cheeks, "I know, I've been busy stitching dresses, it's the demanding season for a seamstress!" she said cheerily.

"Ah, I'm glad to hear it, you'll be opening your own shop in no time."

They shared a knowing grin before he glanced apprehensively at his father behind the counter.

"Come on, you can help me unload the potatoes while you wait for your father," he offered. Abigail happily followed Miles to the crates of vegetables stacked up by the door. He made a show of picking one up and trying to lift it above his head, making her laugh with the exaggerated grunts.

The wooden boxes were far too heavy for her so she held the door open while Miles fetched the crates from outside and placed them under the shelf ready to unpack them. She felt Jerome's eyes upon her again as she stood there and she made a point of not looking in his direction. She couldn't stand the way he looked at her.

Once the crates were all inside, they knelt down to empty them. She chatted away with Miles as they worked side by side, restocking the empty shelves with the potatoes and carrots. By the time they were done, Abigail's father emerged from the back of the shop, stifling a yawn as he said goodnight to Jerome.

Abigail got to her feet, dusting off the dirt from her hands and Miles reached over to give her a hug goodbye. As she grabbed her groceries and went to join her father, she caught Jerome glaring in her and Miles's direction. The man looked furious at their brief display of affection. Blushing slightly, she averted her eyes and muttered a polite goodnight to him before leading the way out of the shop to hold the door open for her father so that he could navigate his walking stick with ease.

"I'll expect you at the crack of dawn tomorrow morning, Garth!" Jerome barked out.

"Yes, boss," her father called out as the pair of them finally headed home, their stomachs rumbling after their gruelling day of work.

ABIGAIL'S DAYS passed in a similar manner; working long hours, having a laugh with Miles as she bought her groceries and cooking a good meal for her and her father in the evening. On a particularly nice evening, Abigail returned home but she didn't feel like staying in. "Shall we go for a little look outdoors? It's such a nice evening," she asked her father.

"Oh, I don't think I'm up for it tonight but you go ahead if you like," he said.

Abigail took in his sad smile, wondering what it would take to see him truly joyful. He seemed to fixate a lot on their hardship, rather than trying to see the good things. Even if those things were small slivers of happy moments.

PUSHING THE DEPRESSING THOUGHT ASIDE, she sliced up some cold ham for her father along with thick slices of the fresh bread she'd brought home from the bakery before buttoning up her coat ready to leave.

"Be careful, Abi," her father warned, peering out the window.

"It's still daylight, Father," she pointed out, "but I will, don't worry."

As she opened the front door, she almost barrelled straight into Miles. He was standing with his arm raised as if he was about to knock on the door.

"Miles," she laughed, "what good timing." Now she could invite him out for a walk with her for some quality time together.

"Hi, Abigail." His tone was subdued, not at all like his usual self.

Concerned, she took in his facial expression; his lips were turned down and his eyes were devoid of their usual shine.

"Miles, what's wrong?" she asked, her heart racing slightly in worry.

"My father is sending me away," he stated. Eventually, he raised his gaze to look at her, as if it was painful to do so.

"What?" What do you mean sending you away?" A horrible tight feeling took hold of her chest.

"He says that I'm a good for nothing dreamer and I need to learn a thing or two about hard work. He's planning to send me to my uncle's farm to become a farm hand." Miles sighed sadly as he spoke.

"But...but..." Abigail had no words. This couldn't be happening. It couldn't. She couldn't imagine her life without Miles. They'd become so close this summer and she always looked forward to seeing him at the end of the day; in the shop, helping him with errands, going for walks and playing one of their games. What was she going to do?

"Abigail," some fire returned to his voice as he took both her hands in his. "I have to leave tonight if I ever want to be independent without him controlling my life," he said urgently.

"But where are you going to go?" Abigail choked out the words as she tried to stop tears from welling up in her eyes.

"I don't know. But I'm going to let him think that I'm following his commands and pretend that I'm leaving quickly to avoid any difficult goodbyes. By the time he gets word that I haven't shown up at the farm, I'll be long gone."

"Oh, Miles, I can't believe this." Abigail could no longer hold back the tears and he drew her in for a hug. She clung on, praying that she could somehow change his mind, that he wouldn't have to go.

"This is my only chance to follow my dream," his voice was suddenly thicker as he spoke into her ear, "and get away from my father. Maybe one day I'll be able to return and I'll come back for you." He drew away slowly. "But for now, I have to say goodbye. Before he gets suspicious."

"I don't know what to say." How was she supposed to say goodbye to Miles?

"Goodbye, Abigail," he turned abruptly, hiding his face from her, and walked away.

Frozen with shock, she stood there for a long time, unable to move, trying to process what had just happened. Something seemed a little off; Jerome Walter had always dismissed Miles's dream of becoming a solicitor, insisting it was nonsense, but he'd always been so set on Miles working in the shop and eventually taking it over when Jerome retires. Why would he suddenly send him away?

Eventually, she quietly opened the door to their tiny apartment after wandering around aimlessly, oblivious to the rain that had soaked her hair, clothes and shoes.

"Abigail, where have you been?" her father

demanded, pushing himself to standing with his stick. His expression grew worried as he took in her appearance, hobbling across the room as fast as he could. "What's happened?"

"Oh, Father," she choked, bursting into tears at the sight of his concern. As he held her like he used to do when she was little, she managed to get the words out, that Miles was leaving, his father sending him away. She kept the rest quiet, about his plans to run away, not wanting any hint to get back to Jerome.

"I'm sorry, Abi, I know he's always been a very good friend to you."

Gradually, her sobs eased up and she reached out for a handkerchief to wipe up the stray tears.

"You're shivering, it's a good thing I stoked up the fire." Letting her go, her father got her sat in front of the fire to dry off while he used his walking stick to get up and fetch her a clean nightdress and pair of socks from the cupboard. As she shed her wet clothes, the feel of warm, dry ones was so soothing, especially wrapping up her freezing cold feet in a pair of thick woollen socks.

"Come on, let's get you to bed. A good night's sleep

can cure the worst of life's pain," her father encouraged. Gently, he wrapped a blanket around her shoulders and brewed a cup of flowery smelling tea for her to drink. It was much more bitter than she expected, just like life, wrinkling her nose she took another sip.

"It'll soothe you and help you to sleep, try and drink it up." For once, her father took care of her instead of the other way around, making the bed for her and tucking her in, kissing her forehead goodnight.

"Goodnight," Abigail whispered, her eyes closed as she imagined it was Miles she was talking to. It was a long time before she finally fell asleep, her dreams filled with longing and disappointment.

7

THE PROPOSAL

The days all blended into one after Miles was gone. She'd taken to shopping at a different greengrocer, no longer able to bear the sight of Walter's without him pottering about with that perpetual cheery smile. Now it was just filled with the sight of Jerome's lecherous gaze, leaving her uncomfortable and sick to her stomach. She hated him even more now, as the reason Miles was gone.

After a couple of weeks, she took her usual morning walk to work. Summer was well and truly over; the air having cooled and the leaves were turning brown ready to disappear until next year. If only she could hide herself away, the onset of Autumn felt bleak and empty without Miles to share it with.

This was silly, there was nothing she could do so she shook off the chill as she stepped through the door to Mrs Hardcastle's Haberdashery. The familiar sound of the bell above the door jangling lifted her spirits for a moment. She enjoyed the job and this year would be easier for she had permanent work.

She called out good morning and headed to pass by the counter to the back of the shop as usual. Already her mind was on the lacy hem she needed to finish before sorting out the new stock that arrived yesterday. Once that was done the place would be nice and organised. Mrs Hardcastle hated being unable to find something.

An arm flung out and stopped her in her tracks however.

Confused, Abigail looked up at Mrs Hardcastle whose expression was like ice. She folded her arms and spoke, "You are no longer welcome in my shop, I'm afraid I'm going to have to ask you to leave."

Abigail froze, her mouth hung open in confusion. Surely this must be a joke.

However, Mrs Hardcastle's face was set in a serious line and she didn't budge from her barring stance.

"Please, Mrs Hardcastle, I... I haven't done anything wrong," she begged, confused about the sudden turn of events.

"I cannot have a harlot like you working for me. I have a reputation to uphold."

"Wh...wha...?" Abigail could not believe such an insult. *Harlot? What on earth was she talking about?*

"I've not got time to argue this. Now, out with you!" Mrs Hardcastle waved a hand towards the door like she was trying to shoo her out.

"But..." Abigail began, trying to understand what was going on here. There must have been a terrible misunderstanding.

"Are you deaf? Get out! I've a customer on his way and I don't want my shop to be seen entertaining the likes of you."

Abigail felt winded with shock and embarrassment as she turned around to reach for the door.

Before she could open it however, the bell tinkled and a heavy boot stomped in to the shop. She looked up to see the smug face of Jerome Walter smirking at her.

"Ah, good morning, Mr Walter," Mrs Hardcastle said pointedly, "I have your jacket ready to collect."

"Why, thank you, Mrs Hardcastle," he practically purred before fixing his eyes on Abigail in his usual manner. "And nice to see you, Abigail, it's been a while since you've come around," he said suggestively with a slow grin.

Feeling utterly ashamed, she gave him a tight smile before continuing to leave the shop, feeling Mrs Hardcastle's disapproving looks boring into her. She hadn't even closed the door behind her before she heard her former employer loudly apologise for Abigail's presence:

"I'm terribly sorry, Mr Walter, I must thank you for alerting me about the girl and her questionable exploits."

How could he? Her heart hammered as shock coursed through her body. *He* had told Mrs Hardcastle that she was a... a common prostitute! Was this punishment for her avoiding his shop? His way to get her fired? Or did this have something to do with Miles and making sure he was putting as big a divide as possible between them? She simply couldn't believe it, that someone could be so despicable. If this was what he was capable of then she was glad that Miles had escaped from his grasp, away from his foul presence.

Only now she had a bigger problem... whatever was she to do?

Her bafflement led her to loop around several streets without paying attention to where she was going. Before long, she realised she was in Mr Samuel's pickpocketing territory. Perhaps this was a sign of where her life was headed. No longer in the direction of her long-awaited fantasy where her and Miles got married and she opened her own seamstress shop... now she would be working as a thief for a shady character like Mr Samuel.

Sure enough, she spotted Zackery across the square, walking close behind a gentleman, his attention fixated on his mark. For one wild moment she considered running over there to join in, taking Mr Samuel up on his previous offer.

No, this can't be the only solution. I'm not going to

survive by robbing innocent strangers and being constantly indebted to his criminal gang.

Quickly, she turned the other way before Zackery spotted her. As she walked through the streets towards home, she felt a prickle of paranoia. Mrs Hardcastle's words were still ringing in her head; *I cannot have a harlot like you working for me.* Suddenly, every look from a passing stranger was echoing her humiliating dismissal. She looked down at her new cotton dress, the one she'd spent a week stitching together with leftover scraps of fabric in the shop. The day she'd finished it and tried it on she'd been so proud, finally feeling like a pretty young woman, hoping that Miles would see her wearing it and see her differently; as more than a friend, no longer a little girl.

Did the dress make her look like a harlot? Or had Mrs Hardcastle noticed that she'd used fabrics from her shop and saw it as stealing? Perhaps she ought to go back and explain that she'd only used scraps that had been thrown out, that she'd never dream of stealing.

It was no use. Mrs Hardcastle had made it clear that she was no longer welcome. Once the woman had made up her mind about something, there was no changing it. She always reiterated that she had no tolerance for nonsense and she had probably already told everyone she'd come into contact with about the apparent scandal.

Abigail could never show her face there again.

Her heart sunk as the reality hit her. However was she going to make it as a seamstress now? She had no other contacts, no prospects for another job and soon, no money.

Oh, Miles, how I wish you were here to talk to.

There was nowhere left to go but home and tell her father of her disappointment. What were they going to do? What was she going to say to him?

"That darned man," her father had quite a few choice words to say about Jerome after Abigail arrived home, her head hanging as she explained what had happened at the shop.

"I'm sorry, Father." There wasn't anything else she could say. She'd let him down, she'd let them both down.

"It's not your fault, Abigail," he sighed, sitting down

and sinking his head into his hands. She knew deep down that it wasn't her fault, but it still made her feel utterly lousy and useless.

"What are we going to do?" she asked. Looking up at her, he started to talk.

"I've had an idea. Jerome Walter has asked for your hand in marriage. You'll be well provided for being married to a merchant such as him, with no shortage of food and a warm bed to sleep in. Then, when I'm gone, you'll have someone to look after you. Well, even before I'm gone...

"You deserve a better life than this, Abigail, and if I can't give it to you then take this chance. He's made a very enticing offer, seems that he's had his eye on you for a long time. And if your friend, Miles ever comes back then you'll be family and get to spend all the time you like with him."

Abigail froze, utterly stunned into silence at her father's words. *Marry. Jerome. Was he kidding?*

Unfortunately, his face was deadly serious, his eyes defeated.

"Father, there has to be another option."

He shook his head. "What's that? Going out to beg on the streets until you find another job? Spending another winter going hungry and having to spend all your time looking after me when I'm poorly?"

"But, Father, I'd much rather do those things than marry Jerome."

"The matter is settled, Abigail, this is your only chance for a safe a future."

"No, I won't do it. I hate that man, Father, he's awful. He forced Miles to leave town, and it was him that got me fired from Mrs Hardcastle's, I know it," she argued, feeling a sick twist of anger and dread.

"I'm not Mr Walter's biggest fan either, but he can provide for you in ways that I can't. Abigail, we have no choice."

She felt her cheeks flush with anger. How could he have agreed to this behind her back? And knowing what Jerome was like? She felt like nothing more than an object being sold to the highest bidder. *Well, you know what, I do have a choice.*

"No, no, I won't do it. Please don't make me do this," she felt tears well up, blurring her vision. She may as well be doomed to a life on the streets.

Wiping her eyes, she looked at her father. His face was resigned, he'd already made up his mind.

"Abigail..." he began, in a tone that commanded her to listen. There was absolutely nothing he could say that would change her mind.

"No, I'm not marrying Jerome Walter!" she yelled.

"He will be here soon to speak with us, perhaps if you listened to what he has to say then you'll see the benefit of the situation," he argued.

Her breathing hitched and a cold chill shot through her. *He was coming here?* How could her father do such a thing... only she knew he was worried about his own health. About what would happen to her when he passed. It didn't matter, some things were worse than death. This was not the answer.

In a panic, she grabbed her coat and made for the door. If she left quickly then she could avoid having to see his horrid controlling expression, grinning away like he'd finally cornered her.

"Abigail, where are you going? Come back here!" Her father's shouts echoed down the hallway as she took off running. She'd already said what she had to say. There was no way she was going to consider marrying Jerome Walter.

8

THE FAILURE

*A*bigail's earlier burst of determination was beginning to wear off. She'd been so upset with her father and horrified at the idea of becoming Jerome's wife that she had taken off, getting as far away as she possibly could so that they couldn't find her.

Now it was dark and she was cold and hungry, with no idea where to go next. For a brief moment she longed for Miles to magically appear, he always knew just what to do in bad situations. *But Miles is gone. Wishing he would appear isn't going to help me figure this out.*

She found herself walking down by the Thames, where the two of them used to spend time during the warm summer months. Back then the sight of it felt full of promise. Now it just felt bleak, empty and imposing shrouded in darkness. The path was eerily quiet and a prickle of fear took hold as she considered her situation. She really ought to find somewhere safe and less exposed. It hadn't been that long since the spate of Jack the Ripper killings.

Her heart hammered as she hurried along the path back towards the main road, convinced that every looming shadow was a predator. *Why did I have to think about those murders right now?* Something darted out in front of her and she screamed out loud... but it was only a rat. Even so, it gave her such a fright that she ran the rest of the way, not stopping until she reached the cobbled street up ahead, lined with street lamps emitting reassuring pools of light.

As she panted, trying to get her breath back, one or two carriages passed by but the area was rather quiet apart from the rhythmic clip-clopping of horse's hooves on the cobblestones. She straightened up, intending to walk towards Oxford Circus. She had no idea what she was going to do once she got there but if she just kept moving then maybe a solution would come to her. If anything, it felt like a good idea to be somewhere more highly populated, and further away from the depravity of East London.

Before she could move any further however, a shadow loomed over her and the metallic taste of fear flooded her mouth once more, freezing her to the spot.

"Why, good evening, Abigail, I didn't expect to see you out here at this hour."

Her dread thickened as she recognised Zackery for the second time that day, taking in his smug smile.

"Yes, well, life is just full of surprises, isn't it," she shot back, having reached her limit for politeness after the day she'd had.

"And a bit of fire in you, this is certainly a change," he commented, looking her up and down as if he was drinking in the sight of her.

Though her skin crawled, she just shot him an exasperated look.

"What do you want, Zackery?" She sighed.

"Come now, I'm just saying hello. I can hardly leave a young lady out here all by herself."

"Well, my day couldn't get any worse at this point," she sighed, giving in to Zackery's sweeping gesture to follow him.

With no other options in sight, she fell into step with Zackery. He was explaining that the spot where he sleeps was just a few streets away.

As they walked, Abigail didn't say much, trying to process everything in her mind instead. The humiliating dismissal at Mrs Hardcastle's Haberdashery this morning, the argument with her father, the insistence she marry a man she loathed and now having run away she was faced with spending the night on the streets of London with a pickpocket. How her luck had changed in less than one day.

"Here we are," Zackery swept his arm out, indicating the underside of a bridge.

Abigail hadn't been paying attention to their route so she didn't even know where they were. Not that she cared at this point.

"Come, sit down," he insisted. The area was completely empty and he reached out for a battered knapsack, pulling out a blanket and a rag or two. He arranged the rags on the ground, gesturing for her to sit. Once they were settled, he wrapped the blanket around her shoulders. It was surprisingly thick and eased her shivering slightly.

Next, he produced a pie, which he unwrapped carefully. "I stole this from the bakery earlier. I managed to get two so this one's left over," he passed it to her, "here, eat up."

She was too hungry to argue, her stomach giving off a loud rumble at the smell of the pastry which was still light and fresh. She took a large bite, tasting the slightly sweet, tangy burst of apple. Once she'd eaten her fill, she looked back up at him. It was certainly a surprise for him to be showing her kindness like this, it was the opposite of what she would have expected.

In the dim light he was watching her patiently and gave her a slight smile as their eyes met.

"Thanks," she said awkwardly.

"Well, I couldn't just let a lady starve, now could I?"

She gave him a tight smile in return.

"So, what's your story, darlin'?" he asked, his usual direct manner having softened slightly.

She took a deep breath and launched into telling him about how poor her and her father were. Feeling a flush of pride as she explained that she'd been doing well working as a seamstress... until Jerome Walter had sent Miles away and ruined everything. Once she got talking, it all came pouring out, like a waterfall she had no chance of stopping. Eventually, she got up to the part about her father trying to force her to marry Jerome Walter, leading her to run away.

She finally finished her story, leaning back against the wall of the bridge, worn out as if she'd been running for miles. It felt good to let it all out however.

Zackery let out a long, low whistle. "That's one hell of a day."

He moved slightly closer, passing a stoneware jug of drink over to her.

Peering at it, she took a sniff and wrinkled her nose at the strong smell of the liqueur, shaking her head and holding it back out to him.

"Go on, have a couple of sips. It'll calm you down and warm you up. 'Sides, a little drink won't do no harm," he insisted. "How do you think I survive out on the streets in the cold?"

She considered him for a moment. The urge to make herself feel better and escape her worries propelled her to take a sip.

"Urrrgh," she squealed, screwing up her face and cringing at the foul taste of it. Zackery let out a low chuckle.

"First time, huh? Come on, a little bit more, it gets better after the first couple of sips."

She raised her eyebrows, not entirely convinced. *Why not? I may as well get the full effects of this awful stuff.* Gearing herself up, she took another swig, holding her breath and gulped down another couple of sips.

"eeeergh," she shook her head, shoving the bottle back at Zackery, well and truly done with it. This time however, she felt herself let out a slight giggle and a slow warmth spread through her. *Perhaps he was right about one thing.*

"That's the stuff." He grinned before knocking back the bottle and taking a generous couple of swigs.

"You can always stay on the streets you know," he began. "There's a good living to be made picking pockets. You could make more than the pennies you'd get for a full day in that sewing shop in one hour. Think of the freedom you'd have, no one telling you what to do, no getting fired or having to marry some old miser."

Perhaps it was the drink talking, but the freedom did sound nice right about now and she was in no place to turn down the prospect of money.

"I'll teach you everything I know, we'll be a team, unstoppable."

For a brief moment she considered it, until reality came crashing down as a gust of bitter wind hit them, blowing away any momentary madness as a result of the vile liquor.

What on earth am I doing? Sitting under a bridge with creepy Zackery. She'd always held on to the hope that Miles would come back and that everything would be okay again but as she faced spending the night out here, it felt like that hope had now been shattered.

Feigning tiredness, Zackery left her to snuggle up in

the blanket as best she could. It was cold, dark, scary but she closed her eyes, trying to imagine that she was only on the floor back home. That the fire had died out and she'd wake up in the morning and light it to make the tea as usual. Another gust of wind blew over her, a sharp reminder that she was a long way from home.

Feeling lonelier than she'd ever felt in her life, she silently let the tears that had been building up inside of her fall down her cheeks, considering the failure of her life until she eventually fell asleep.

9

THE END OF ALL

*T*he thoroughfares of London were all hustle and bustle as she followed Zackery through his shortcut of alleyways and narrow streets.

"This is how you get out quickly without being caught. You can be out in the open of Oxford Street one minute and ducking out of sight to emerge in Soho the next before your mark has even noticed his pockets are a little lighter."

They'd been up at the crack of dawn, Zackery explaining that some of his best work was done first thing in the morning; 'before people even know what hit them.'

Mr Samuel had clearly trained him well for he seemed to know all the best hiding spots and escape routes, who to avoid, who to target and which domain belonged to them.

"Don't ever cross the Thames and begin working that side, that's Charlie's territory. You can do no worse than step on another gang's toes," he explained, his tone serious.

"The key thing to remember is to be subtle. Blend in. If you nick someone's wallet and then take off running it's a dead giveaway. But if you slide it into your own pocket and keep walking as if nothing happened then there's nothing to indicate anything untoward has happened. Piece of cake."

They stopped walking and Zackery turned her around to survey the street from their vantage point of the library steps. They had to take care not to stand too close to the door to save being shouted at by the librarians inside.

"Now, select your target," he ordered.

Heart pounding, she tried to scan the crowd like he taught her. Telling herself that she'd get away from this as soon as she could. If she didn't steal anything herself then maybe it wouldn't be wrong.

She saw an older man striding out of a nearby doorway and felt a jolt of panic for he looked just like Jerome. *Has he tracked me down? Come to drag me back home and force my hand?* As she got a better look at him however, her shoulders dropped and she let go of the breath she'd been holding in sheer relief. It wasn't him at all, just a stranger.

He had the same looming presence as Jerome however, and Abigail watched as the man fixated his gaze on a lady passing him by in the street, reaching his arm out to grab her.

"Him," Abigail spoke with venom as she pointed right at the Jerome look-a-like.

Zackery gave a cheerful nod, "Nice. Watch and learn m'lady."

Abigail stayed put, as instructed, leaning on one of the large, ornate stone pillars in front of the library's doorway. She watched Zackery slouch off, his head down, hands in pockets, looking completely nondescript. Soon he was gaining on the man, trailing behind him fairly closely. If Abigail hadn't been paying such close attention to Zackery's movements, she would have missed the quick twitch of his hand moving from his pocket to the man's, and back again.

Soon he had hurried past the man before crossing the road, frowning like he was deep in thought. He disappeared and when Abigail was beginning to wonder if he had just left her there, he materialised on her other side, seemingly out of nowhere.

"Good, right?" he asked, grinning from ear to ear and waving the stolen wallet triumphantly.

"Well done," she said heavily. Despite how much the man reminded her of Jerome and his leering over that girl, it still didn't feel right being involved, however indirectly, in robbing him. Didn't Zackery ever wonder if what he did was wrong?

She trailed around after him for the rest of the morning, watching as he expertly stole from unsuspecting passers-by. For the last mark of the day, he insisted that she get involved by walking alongside him, arm in arm as if they were a young couple.

"It's the perfect disguise. Besides, nobody would suspect you. At least not yet anyway," he laughed.

"What's that supposed to mean?" She frowned, not understanding what he was getting at.

"You're still innocent and fresh. Just wait until you've been on the streets a few weeks." His voice was full of arrogance and she felt repulsed by it, wanting to wriggle free from his arm but he had an almost iron grip on her.

As they approached the lady that Zackery had identified as their next target, Abigail's heart gave a lurch as she recognised the voluminous dress she was wearing. It was one that she had worked on in Mrs Hardcastle's shop. It was a lovely sky-blue colour and she remembered spending hours on the stitching to create the ruched effect around the skirt so that it would fall just right.

How ironic that now she was faced with stealing from the very same dress she so proudly helped to make.

Feeling sick to her stomach as Zackery steered her in the woman's direction. "I don't think I want to do this," she hissed at him.

"Bit late to back out now," he snapped back.

"Zackery, no!" Her outburst was loud enough that the woman heard her, turning to look over her shoulder at the exact moment Zackery reached out for her purse.

Immediately she screamed out, "Thieves, thieves!" which started a chorus of scandalised gasps and shouts. Before Abigail could comprehend just what was going on, Zackery yanked at her arm as he started to run.

"Oi! Stop right there!" A very tall police officer was running full pelt towards Zackery, catching up to him in just a few strides, all but tackling him to the ground and leaving Abigail frozen to the spot in shock.

The lady in the blue dress shrieked, causing two gentlemen nearby to rush to her assistance where she began babbling in a high-pitched voice about how she'd been minding her own business when these two street urchins had snatched up her purse and attempted to make off with it.

"Good day, Miss, I'm terribly sorry about this ordeal," the police officer cut in, tipping his hat with one hand and holding Zackery in handcuffs with the other. He was wriggling around like mad but the police officer's grip was so tight there was no room to budge. "My name is Officer Jack Bart."

"Well, thank goodness you came to the rescue, Officer," the woman started talking in a simpering voice, "otherwise these tramps would have made off with my purse which contains rather a lot of valuables, not to mention the purse itself was hand stitched by Mrs Rose of the Rose Petal Boutique. It cost a small fortune!"

"Well, don't you worry, Ma'am, these two will be punished accordingly," Jack Bart assured her. As he spoke, Abigail realised that they were talking about her too, thinking that she'd intended to steal from her.

"No... you've got it all wrong, I wasn't-" Jack Bart cut her off before she could finish explaining.

"That's enough," he barked, grabbing her by the arm, "I'm taking you both to the station!" He whirled her around and began marching them in the opposite direction. Abigail could hear nothing but disgusted comments from the surrounding crowd amongst more loud exclamations from the lady wearing her dress. She was making sure that everyone in a ten-foot radius knew the details of her attempted mugging.

Abigail's face burned with shame as she practically ran to keep up with the officer's long stride. They seemed to attract plenty of looks on their way to the police station, people muttering about common street thieves and whores and all sorts of things as they passed by. She'd never felt so humiliated in all her life and she knew her father would be so disappointed in her. Perhaps she should have went along with his plan to marry Jerome after all. Surely, anything would be better than this.

After they arrived at the station, Officer Bart pushed them both into a room, slamming the heavy door behind him. He gestured for Abigail to sit down, keeping hold of Zackery until his hands were tied around the back of the chair so that there was no way he could escape. His easy going, friendly manner was gone and now he acted like he barely knew Abigail at all, like she was nothing more than a passing rodent in the street.

The police officer got them to state their names,

addresses and occupations. Zackery had short, curt replies like he'd done this before but Abigail stumbled over her answers, trying to explain how she'd come to run away from home.

"How old are you, Miss?" His tone seemed to soften as he looked at her, listening to her fearful sounding answers.

"Almost sixteen Sir."

"And can you tell me what happened?" he asked rather gently.

"Well, like I said, I'd run away from home after that argument with my father," she began, trying to speak clearly so that he'd understand. "Then I ran into Zackery. I, er, I guess I didn't... didn't know where else to go, what else to do, it was so late and I was cold and hungry..." she stumbled over her words before Officer Bart interrupted her.

"I mean about the robbery that occurred today," he countered.

"Oh, well, I was walking with Zackery and-"

"Look, we both did it, that loud-mouthed posh lady told ya already. Whatever she's about to say, don't listen. She's a pickpocket just like me, playing her part of the innocent little girl," Zackery practically spat out the words as he interrupted her version of the story.

"No, that's not true! I didn't want to steal anything, I refused. I told him that it wasn't right and I didn't want to be a part of it. It was him that took the purse, not me!"

The officer looked from one of them to the other, slowly assessing them before he spoke.

"Zackery Green, you are under arrest for theft. Mr Roger here will escort you to the cells." He gave a sharp rap on the window to their right and promptly, the door opened and another officer, presumably Mr Roger, entered. Jack simply nodded at Zackery and Mr Roger had him up and out of his seat in an instant, steering him with considerable force through the door, letting it swing shut behind him.

"Now, Abigail..." Officer Bart said, turning his attention to her. "I ought to have you thrown in the poor house for stealing."

"But, Sir!" she exclaimed, but he held up a hand to stop her before she could get started.

"I don't need to hear it. Whether or not you had intent to steal, you were still involved with that young man at the time the crime was committed. It's obvious you're no street urchin, you don't have the hardened savvy about you like the rest of them. What did you say your last name was?" He asked.

"P-Patrick. Abigail Patrick." Her voice trembled as she spoke, utterly terrified about what was going to happen next. Imagine this got into the papers. First, she was accused of being a harlot at Mrs Hardcastle's and now this... She'd stand no chance of ever getting anywhere with her life. Her chance at a good future was over.

Jack Bart nodded, leaning back in his chair to stand up again. "Right, come with me." He grabbed her by the arm, not quite as tightly as before and marched her out of the room and down a dismal, dark corridor which smelled faintly of urine.

They stopped in front of a small, empty jail cell. Abigail began to reel in horror, *no, no, no, no, no, this can't be happening. I can't be going to jail!*

But sure enough, the officer unlocked the cell door

and swung it open pushing her in and locking the door closed again.

"Please, you can't leave me here!" She cried out, as she started to sob uncontrollably.

"You'll be behind bars until I decide what to do with you. Just count yourself lucky I didn't throw you into a cell with all the others."

After he turned on his heel and strode away, Abigail collapsed onto the floor and made no effort to try and stop her tears. Her life was over. This was it, she'd gone from having a loving father, a roof over her head and work where she had ambition to being thrown into a jail cell. There was no coming back from this.

10

AN OLD FRIEND

*A*bigail woke in the morning, her body stiff and cold from spending the night in a freezing cold cell with nothing in the way of comfort. There wasn't even a blanket to sleep under, it was utterly dismal. She'd cried until her tears ran dry, finally falling asleep after exhausting herself with emotion.

Now her mouth was dry and her head was pounding from the combination of Zackery's foul liqueur, the lack of food and water and all the exertion from the previous day. She couldn't have been in here for 24 hours yet but it felt like a lifetime already. However was she to survive in this foul place?

Slowly, she uncurled herself from the foetal position on the floor and stiffly sat up to take in her surroundings. There wasn't much to look at; the grey concrete walls, solid iron bars to keep her locked in and a filthy, chipped bedpan in the corner. There was no window. The only indication she had of the fact it was now daylight came from the corridor outside her cell where a distant window let the sunlight through. It felt so far away, like she'd never be able to reach it again. *Oh, God, what if I'm stuck here forever? Father doesn't know where I am, I have no way of reaching him. They could send me on to the poorhouse and I'd be separated from Father and Miles and everything forever.*

The tears wanted to fall again but she bit them back and tried to think.

The distant daylight however was a mild comfort in this dark cesspit. The night had been filled with screams; prisoners sending themselves mad with guilt and anger. Some hurled themselves against the bars of their cells in a desperate attempt to break free. Abigail has been utterly terrified at the noises which seemed to come from all directions at first. Eventually, she realised that these people were also locked away just like her, that they couldn't harm her. Fear then turned into despair as she wondered if this was to be her future. Trapped in a jail cell for a crime she didn't commit, yelling and screaming for freedom until it drove her mad.

Just when she started to think she was going to die of thirst, a foreboding looking police officer marched into sight and shoved a cup of water through the bars along with a hard-looking piece of bread. Abigail snatched it up eagerly, gulping down the water with relief.

"Hey, Mister, would it be possible to get some more? Please?" she called out after finishing the cup of water, feeling her parched throat return to normal.

The man acted as if he didn't even hear her, turning on his heel and disappearing down the corridor with a purposeful stride.

Defeated, she dropped down onto the floor again, feeling as insignificant as a rat, picking up the chunk of stale bread and sank her teeth into it. It was extremely dry and unappealing but her empty stomach was not going to discriminate.

Only now, she wished she hadn't drunk her water so quickly. The bread was hard and dry and clogged her throat as she chewed. There was very little water left so she saved the last few drops of liquid in the cup until she was finished eating. It still wasn't enough to quench her thirst and her heart sunk as she thought of the police officer walking away without even acknowledging her. It was no use trying to ask for more, there was nothing for it but to wait.

The minutes stretched by, turning into hours. Abigail drifted off back to sleep, walking with a sudden jerk at the loud clanging noise. Disorientated, she sat up with a start, rubbing the sleep from her eyes.

Officer Bart was outside her cell, holding out a big ring of keys which all jangled against each other.

"Miss Patrick, you're free to go," he announced as he turned the key in the lock with a big click, the big heavy door creaked as he yanked it open.

Afraid but a little elated, Abigail scrambled to her feet, her heart hammering with anticipation and relief.

"I... I can leave?" she squeaked, hardly knowing what to say.

"Your father is here to pick you up," he explained, stepping aside to let her out of the cell.

"My father?" Her eyes swam with tears at these words and she was filled with an overwhelming sense of relief.

Abigail could hardly move fast enough as she kept up with Officer Bart's long strides, ignoring the shouts and catcalls from the cells they passed by. Her only thought was the prospect of freedom and seeing her father again. *However had he found her? This could only be a miracle. But what if this isn't real? What if Father isn't really here?*

Doubt began to swallow her up as she imagined Jerome Walter's face smirking down at her, having pretended to be her father. Getting released from jail only to be imprisoned into a miserable marriage and life as his wife. Dread rose up in her as they approach the door ahead, Abigail praying her fears were not going to come true.

As soon as the officer unlocked the door to his office, Abigail let out an overjoyed yell as she took in the sight of her father leaning against his stick, his face a haggard expression of tiredness. It dissolved into relief as Abigail launched herself across the room into his arms, letting go of her tears and sobbing with regret, joy and utter relief.

"Oh, Abigail, I've been ever so worried. I'm so glad that you are all right, don't you ever do this to me again." He held on to her tightly, rocking her back and forwards slightly like she was a little girl again.

"Father, I'm so very sorry. It's been awful since the moment I left," she gasped, "I promise I didn't steal that lady's purse, all I did was tell Zackery it was wrong and I didn't want to be a part of it."

"I know, Abigail, you are no thief. I told Jack this myself and insisted he release you at once," her father nodded to Officer Bart.

"When you told me your name was Patrick it clicked why you looked so familiar, young lady," Jack explained, "your father and I served together when we were practically still boys. I joined the force just as Garth here met your mother. The four of us used to have dinner and jolly evenings together, your mother, father and my wife and I. You're the spitting image of your mother you are, it's a darned shame what happened.

"I knew I had to get word out and track down your father. It took me all night to find him, things have changed so much over the years. When I knocked on the door, he opened it in a frenzied panic, asking where you were before even noticing it was me. I told him you was here, picked up for pick pocketing. 'Not my Abigail,' he insisted, giving me a piece of his mind before I calmed him down and told him I'd take 'im straight here to get you. That it was my duty as an old friend. That's when it clicked who I was."

"I'm forever grateful, Jack," her father responded. "I don't know what I'd have done otherwise, I've been out of my mind with worry."

Guilt coursed through Abigail as she took in her father's tired, dishevelled appearance. He looked as though he hadn't slept in days and it was all her fault for running out like that without a second thought.

"Oh, Father, I feel awful. I didn't think," she said, her voice wobbling again.

"I should never have tried to force your hand with Jerome Walter, that man is a beast. It was a moment of panic, I let him force me into a corner when I should have stood up to him," he explained.

"I forgive you," Abigail choked as she embraced him.

The door opened once more and Jack Bart appeared again, this time holding Zackery by the arm. Her pick pocketing acquaintance looked utterly nonchalant, like spending a night in jail was no big deal. She supposed that to him it probably wasn't given that he spent most nights sleeping outdoors underneath a bridge.

"Right chap, I'm letting you off with a warning this time but if I so much as catch wind of you prowling about the streets then it's off to the poor house with you," Officer Bart scolded Zackery.

"Yes, and you'll be staying away from my daughter if you know what's good for you," Abigail's father spat out, straightening up as best he could, puffing out his chest and furrowing his brow.

Zackery did nothing but roll his eyes as he was led back out of the office, a sickening smirk on his face. "Right, Garth, I need to get on. I'll see you later in the week," Officer Bart called out as they left the room, "And you stay out of trouble, Missy!"

"I will, thank you, Officer," Abigail said politely, feeling her cheeks flush as the embarrassment of the situation began to sink in now that everything had blown over.

"Come on home, Abi," her father said gently, "I've got a surprise waiting."

11

THE SURPRISE

Abigail looked at her father with disbelief. The prospect of a surprise was not a welcome one right now but she had no energy to argue or question it. She was just so happy to be getting far away from this awful place, wanting nothing more than to just scrub the past couple of days from her mind.

At the moment it was filled with nothing but the worst possible scenarios. Dragging her into some twisted compromise where their lives would change for the better, plenty of food, warmth and money if she would only marry Jerome. Perhaps they'd thought of a way to ease her into it, promises of being able to stay with her father, promises that he'd have no intention of keeping.

The feeling of fire that had taken over her the other night before she fled into the night was now extinguished. It had only been a matter of days but her brief time on the streets had left her exhausted and longing for nothing but the comfort of home. Their home might not be much but she'd grown a whole new appreciation for it. It was their home after all, and it was the best they had.

As they began the walk back, her moment of ecstatic relief withered into tiredness and dreaded acceptance of the fate that lay ahead of her. The carriages on the street and the sound of the horses was luxury she could never afford. They just seemed to point out the terrible circumstance she was in. There was no escape. No matter which corner she turned, Jerome seemed to have a way of knowing about it. It seemed he would not stop until she gave in. Perhaps there was no point in fighting this future, perhaps she should just give in and marry him.

They remained silent for most of the journey, both of them lost in their thoughts. When they reached the front door, Abigail wanted nothing more than to curl up in front of the fire and boil a pan of water for tea. The jail cell had been freezing cold, the only surface to lie down on being the concrete floor, the chill seeping right into her bones, feeling like she would never get warm again. It was its own form of punishment.

As they walked however, Abigail realised she didn't recognise the route they were taking. Had she strayed that far from home while out with Zackery? The surrounding streets were lined with townhouses, devoid of the ragamuffin children and starving families that crowded their neighbourhood. They were a long way from the streets of East London now.

"Father, where are we going?" she asked, as fear and confusion prickled down her arms. They had no business around here and it seemed to be a long detour for her father and his leg to be travelling.

"Ah now, that would spoil the surprise," he said mysteriously, his tone edged with a light-hearted smile which only served to confuse her more.

Soon they stopped outside an unfamiliar door and Garth reached out to knock.

Oh, here we go, Abigail thought, bracing herself for whatever horror was waiting inside.

The door opened and there stood a strange woman Abigail had never seen before. She looked to be in her early to mid-thirties, her blonde hair was fastened up on her head. She was short but round and her face was all smiles as she greeted them and welcomed them inside.

"Abigail, it's nice to finally meet you," she said. "I've heard ever so much about you and I can't tell you how glad I am to see you safe and sound and out of that awful place."

"I... I thank you," Abigail stumbled over her words as they walked down the large hallway. She wanted to ask *'who are you?'* but it felt like a rather rude thing to say and she began to wonder if she should already know who the woman was.

"Oh, of course, you'll be wondering what all this is about," the woman said. "I'm Miles's Auntie Pat and I've someone here who can explain it better than me." She opened the door in front of them and held it open, gesturing for Abigail to enter.

Miles's aunt? But how can that be? Surely.... Her heart was hammering as she gaped at Pat and stepped into the room. There, leaning against the large kitchen counter, was no-one other than Miles himself.

His face broke out into a huge grin as Abigail took in the sight of him. She was stunned for a brief moment before running across the room straight into his arms.

"Miles!" she exclaimed as he embraced her and held her close against his chest. "You're here! I thought I'd never see you again." This was overwhelmingly wonderful. Of all the terrible scenarios she'd concocted in her head, she'd never dared to imagine that something so incredible could possibly happen.

"Abigail, oh, I'm so happy to see you. You've no idea what It's been like being apart from you all this time. I never want that to happen again," he said passionately.

They hugged for a long couple of minutes, Abigail feeling all the sadness and worries from the past months fade away. Miles was here. Everything was going to be okay.

They talked for a long time. Miles explained how he'd run away to his aunt's house and that she'd helped him get set up and he was now studying to become a solicitor. She'd got him some work as an assistant with a nearby solicitor's office too, freeing him from having to work for his father.

"My father's days of controlling me are over, I can finally have a life of my own. Well, we can, together, if you want," Miles said passionately, his eyes blazing as he looked into hers.

"Miles...I..." She hardly knew what to say, what Miles was trying to say to her. She could only feel the butterflies in her stomach, the sweeping feeling of excitement rocketing through her.

"Abigail, I love you," he stood in front of her, taking both her hands in his, "I want to marry you. Will you be my wife?"

Her stomach swooped with joy and her heart fluttered like mad. "Oh, Miles, of course I'll marry you!" she said, feeling her face light up into a smile.

He grinned, looking overjoyed and pulled her gently towards him.

They looked into each other's eyes for a few long moments, her mouth stretching into a smile to match his before their lips met for their first kiss. His lips were soft and warm, his kisses gentle and soothing. It was everything she'd ever dreamed of and more.

Feeling dizzy with happiness as they pulled back from their kiss, Abigail felt as if they'd floated up into the sky, away from everyone else to a world that was just their own. Her cheeks were hot and damp as tears of joy welled up in her eyes and spilled out. It was just so overwhelming. Having fled from home at the prospect of being forced to marry Jerome, spending the night on the streets with Zackery only to land in a jail cell, to her father coming to rescue her and then Miles proposing marriage.

"Are you okay, my love? What's the matter?" Miles frowned with concern.

"I'm just so happy, Miles, I've been dreaming about this for so long. In the worst times I longed for you to come back and make everything okay again but I began to lose hope and now you're here and it's...

it's... just so...." She could hardly get the words out as the tears began to trickle down her cheeks once more, "perfect," she finally choked out.

"Abigail, you have no idea how much I missed you while I was gone. That night I left it broke my heart. I almost turned back again but knowing I had the chance to make both our dreams come true and escape my father so that we could have a life on our own was the thing that kept me going. I've been longing for this day for so long."

Their lips met once more, just briefly, but that touch said more than words. Then he wrapped his arms around her, pulling her into a gentle embrace.

It felt so comforting that Abigail felt her frayed nerves start to calm down. It was like she'd stepped into a clean, hot bath.

The tears were gone and she was filled with a mixture of calm and joy as the door behind them opened and her father and Miles's aunt came in. Both of them were smiling expectantly.

Miles tugged on Abigail's hand, pulling her round so that they were stood next to each other, united.

"Abigail and I are to be married," Miles announced.

"Well, isn't that good news!" her father exclaimed, a smile breaking out on his face as he limped forwards to shake Miles's hand and give Abigail a hug.

"Well now, this is all very well and good but you must wait until Abigail is at least sixteen," Pat intervened.

"I can wait as long as it takes," Miles said simply.

"Until then, Garth and Abigail can live here with us," she announced.

This sparked an exclamation of surprise and feeble protest from Abigail's father who was not used to being shown kindness or a helping hand. Although it was clear he was not complaining at the chance to live in this grand house instead of their tiny, grotty apartment.

"With that leg, you can hardly get by on your own and it's bound to be putting a lot of pressure on Abigail to provide and care for you. No wonder she's like a grown woman at such a young age. Besides, I could do with the company and it's not proper for a lady such as myself to live alone without a man or family," Pat argued, the matter settled.

"Well, in that case, we'd be delighted."

Abigail grinned at her father's response, taking in the expansive kitchen and beautiful surroundings. This was a far cry from their one-roomed apartment. Here there was an entire room just for cooking and who knew what else.

"Come on, my dear, I'll show you around to let you get your bearings," Pat said to Abigail.

Abigail followed Pat around the house. The downstairs was made up of the kitchen, dining room and two reception rooms and a parlour with a cosy fireplace and plush looking chairs. There was a piano in the corner, something Abigail had never seen before.

"I'll teach you to play, it's a fine skill for a young lady to have," Pat insisted.

Abigail was thrilled with delight to discover that the stairs led to another part of the house. *It had two floors!* It was simply marvellous. Pat showed her to a room at the end of the upstairs hallway. Abigail gasped out loud, it was the most beautiful room she'd ever seen.

A full-sized bed sat in the middle, made up with pretty pink satin sheets, the pillows adorned with matching bows and ribbons. A large dressing table was set up by the window, with a round shiny mirror lined with flowers. An ornate hair brush sat on the surface of the table next to a China pot filled with hairpins and accessories. There was a gorgeous sky-blue vase filled with fresh flowers perched on the side to finish it off.

The huge window was lined with deep pink curtains showing off an expansive view of London, rows and rows of rooftops stretching for miles. Abigail was absolutely stunned. She'd never seen anything so lavish and beautiful.

"This is to be your room," Pat said gently.

Abigail turned to face her, her mouth hanging open in surprise. "Oh, my goodness, this is simply beautiful. Thank you so much."

Pat smiled indulgently. Simply saying thank you didn't seem like enough, but Abigail hardly knew what else she could do to thank her for such generosity.

"There's no use in having a home like this if I have no-one to share it with," Pat said in a light-hearted manner before they began to make their way back downstairs.

Miles and her father were chatting away companionably as Abigail and Pat entered the room again.

"Miles and I were just discussing how we should go back to the apartment and collect our things, Abigail, he reckons there's no time like the present," Garth said, his voice cheery and upbeat.

"I agree," Pat said, "but you really ought to rest your leg, Garth. Miles, why don't you accompany Abigail to collect their things and Garth you can help me with the dinner."

Pat had a way of organising everyone around her without being too pushy. Soon, Abigail and Miles were setting off home, to say goodbye before leaving it forever.

As they arrived, Abigail pushed the door open and was struck by how much smaller it seemed in comparison to the big, fancy townhouse she'd just come from. It was like a whole different world. Miles had talked as they walked, telling her more about his time away and what his aunt was like. She spent the summer months out in the country but she'd had an extended stay out there after losing her husband-to-be in the war. This was her first time back in the city for two years and he reassured Abigail that she was glad of the company from them all.

It didn't take long for Abigail to pack up their scanty belongings. Miles helped her to bundle up their clothes and Abigail carefully wrapped up the picture of her mother, tucking it inside her jacket. She took one last look around, feeling a mixture of sadness and relief. This place may have been one of hardship and many hungry nights, but it had still been a home with a warm fireplace when they needed it the most.

Before leaving, Abigail wrote out a note for the landlord to explain that they had left, sticking it to the door before closing it behind them, turning away to move forward to a new chapter of her life.

As they turned off to the main road to begin the long

walk back to Pat's, well, their new home, a familiar voice sounded behind them.

"Miles, what on earth d'you think you're doing?" They turned around to see Jerome Walter, Miles's father, thundering towards them, his face twisted up in anger. A sharp stab of fear flooded through Abigail at the sight of him.

"I don't see how that's any of your business, Father," Miles said sharply.

"Don't you dare talk back to me. Just where the hell have you been? You made me look like a fool when you didn't show up at the farm like I promised. And you go gallivanting off god-knows-where with this harlot without an explanation and now you stand here giving me lip? I won't be having it, now back to the shop with you!"

"I won't be going anywhere with you, Father. Your days of telling me what to do are over. And I won't have you speaking of my wife-to-be like that." Miles seemed to grow several inches as he straightened up and gave Jerome a piece of his mind.

"You're... you're... what?" Jerome spluttered.

"Abigail and I are to be married as soon as she turns sixteen." Miles spoke calmly.

"I will not allow it, don't you think for one minute that I will—" Jerome began to argue before Miles cut him off again.

"I'm not asking for your permission. I have a job and home of my own where you are not welcome. Now, we'll be going and don't expect to see us any time soon," Miles practically spat out the words, shaking with rage. Before Jerome could get a word in edgeways, Miles spun on his heel, taking Abigail's hand and began to walk away with her.

They were silent for a while as they walked, Abigail not wanting to push him. She felt glad that he'd finally stood up to his beastly father. That they were free of the man's beastly clutches but she also knew it couldn't have been an easy thing for him to do.

"Your apartment was the first place I went when I got back to town, you know," Miles started. "Your father was going out of his mind with worry. He explained what had happened, that my father tried to force your hand, getting you fired from your job, that your father felt like he had no choice, that it seemed like the only option. It was a moment of weakness and he felt awful about putting you in that position."

Abigail felt another stabbing of guilt for making her father feel bad like that but if she hadn't run away then her reality might be very different by now.

"All that is in the past now," Miles said, looking at her with a reassuring smile. "We're together again, we have a nice place to live and a chance to realise our dreams."

Abigail smiled up at him in return, squeezing his hand slightly in agreement. Once again, she revelled in how lucky she was, the reality of the situation having not quite sunk in yet. It may have been the tiredness but she expected to wake up from a dream at any minute now, and find herself back home in front of the fire, listening to her father's hacking cough.

When they finally arrived back at the townhouse, Abigail's father and Pat were sitting comfortably in the living room, glasses of wine in hand and chatting companionably. There was a happy glow in her father's eye, one that she'd never seen before.

"That was quick, did you get everything you needed?" Pat asked, standing up to help them with the bundles of stuff they were carrying.

"Yes, I packed everything that we have. And I left a note for the landlord on the door explaining that we've gone," Abigail told her father.

"Thank you, Abi, that was good thinking," he replied. "Saves me having to send the bloke a letter in the morning."

"Come on, we'll get this stuff up to your rooms and then we can all settle down to dinner," Pat ordered. "Your father's room is on the bottom floor, at the end of the hallway past the stairs." Abigail reached into her jacket to pull out the photograph of her mother but she caught the way that her father was looking at Pat. It was the same wistful expression he wore when he used to tell her stories about her mother.

She tucked the photograph back inside her jacket, instead taking it up to her room to place it above the fireplace, just like it used to be back home. It was a comfort, like she was watching over Abigail. A part of her felt like she was able to show her mother her beautiful new room, that she'd finally found happiness.

Once she'd unpacked and headed downstairs, Pat ordered them all to the kitchen where a huge spread of food was waiting. Abigail gasped out loud at the sight of the whole roast chicken. It must have cost a fortune. Pat had them all carry different dishes through to the dining room which was lit up with candles.

Garth took charge of carving the chicken, passing out generous portions to everyone. There were bowls of steaming hot vegetables and potatoes and a jug of something Abigail had never tried before called gravy. She'd never seen this much food before, it felt like she should be conserving it, eating as little as possible to save the rest to last them the week.

At that moment Miles caught her eye and smiled. As if he understood her thought he shook his head. "Eat all you can," he whispered so no one else would hear.

He was right, this was a different life and she happily tucked in to a full plate of food, watching everyone else enjoying their meal. Pat poured out glasses of wine for everyone. Abigail took a tentative sip, wincing slightly at the strength of it at first. It was nowhere near as foul as the liqueur Zackery shared with her, however.

The evening soon came to an end. Abigail settled into her comfortable new bed with a fireplace of her own, her stomach full and more content than she'd ever been in her life, drifting off to sleep, the start of her day in the jail cell long forgotten.

EPILOGUE - DREAMS

"*I* have your dress ready for you, Miss Peters," Abigail greeted her customer with enthusiasm as she entered the little shop. "Shall we try it on?"

"Oooh, yes please, Mrs Walters!" she exclaimed, jumping up and down on the spot and clapping her hands.

Ann Peters was one of Abigail's favourite customers. She was incredibly chatty and absolutely adored fashion and was always so happy and enthusiastic. They'd had several long talks discussing the latest fashions, who was wearing what and comparing colours and fabrics.

"Oh, please call me Abigail." It felt too formal to have an 18-year-old girl, one her own age, call her Mrs Walters, even if it did still send a little thrill through her to hear someone address her as her married name.

She beckoned Ann to follow her through the back of the shop where her workstation was set up. She had the dress hanging up on display, causing a big audible gasp from Ann who rushed over to it immediately.

"Ooooh, it's simply *gorgeous,*" she gushed, carefully running her hands through the length of it.

Abigail helped her in to the dress for the final fitting. It had to be one of her favourite dresses she'd ever made, rivalling anything that she'd seen from Mrs Hardcastle's Haberdashery. The gown was a delicate pale lilac colour with a ruched neckline. Intricate white roses were sewn from the finest lace and cascaded down the lengths of the skirt, intertwining into a white lace bodice with lilac ribbons patterned around it, meeting at the lower back in a bow.

Ann squealed with delight as she looked in the mirror, twirling around on the spot. "Oh, it's perfect!" she exclaimed, "I'm going to be the belle of the ball!"

"And now you can finally dance with Mr Wright," Abigail teased, knowing how much Ann liked him.

"Perhaps I can," Ann admitted, blushing slightly. "We don't all have the perfect husband like your Miles."

Abigail smiled, feeling proud as ever, running her hand over her rounded belly.

"And you're having a baby, oh, you're just love's young dream," Ann exclaimed, twirling about the floor, her hands clasped against her chest.

"Gosh, Miss Peters, how many of those romance novels have you been reading?" Abigail joked but inside she was thrilled. It was three months until their baby was due and she felt blessed every single day. "Perhaps you'll be starring in one of your own after tonight," Abigail teased.

"Oh, a girl can hope!" Ann said dramatically, clutching her hands to her chest to exaggerate her point before wistfully allowing Abigail to undo the hooks at the back of her dress.

"I hope I'll see you both at the ball tonight," Ann called out from behind the screen as she changed out of her gown and back into her other clothes.

"Oh, I'm sure we'll make an appearance," Abigail said, mentally calculating how many dresses she had left to finish before this evening. "Now, if you'll forgive me, I have a whole row of dresses that still need to be hemmed and finished off before the dance."

"As long as they won't be as beautiful as mine then sew away!" Ann sang out.

Abigail laughed, "I reckon you're wearing my finest work, Miss Peters, don't you worry."

After Abigail carefully wrapped up her dress and took her payment from Ann. The young woman skipped out with a cheery goodbye. Abigail got to work putting the finishing touches to the rest of her creations.

After about an hour, Auntie Pat came through from the front of the house with a cup of tea for the both of them and slices of fruit cake topped with generous helpings of butter and jam.

"How are you getting on, lovie?"

Abigail smiled. Since Pat had set her up with her own shop out the back of the townhouse the pair of them had become very close. She would drop in and help out with some of the basic stitching, chatting away companionably as they worked. Abigail enjoyed the company and found that she had lots of knowledge to pass on to Pat who was always adamant that Abigail was the talent out of the pair of them and her claw-like hands would never be able to keep up.

Now that Abigail was pregnant, Pat was checking on her more and more, ensuring she was getting enough to eat and not overdoing it. They were kept busy until lunchtime, Abigail had hardly noticed the time until the little bell above the door sounded to announce Miles and her father's arrival.

The pair of them were chatting away animatedly, Miles holding the door open so her father could enter with ease. Abigail took in the sight of her father who was looking so much healthier than she'd ever seen him. His clothes were smart, dressed up in a shirt and blazer. While he'd been skin and bone before, he was now broad and had colour in his cheeks, a smile on his face. It lit up at the sight of Pat who stood up to give him a kiss hello. They'd been married for one year now.

"Hello, my love," Miles said, a slow smile breaking out on his face at the sight of her.

Abigail made to stand up but he insisted she stay sitting, leaning down to kiss her hello. After making sure she wasn't working too hard and wasn't tiring herself out, the four of them sat down to eat lunch together in the dining room. It was just a short little walk from the shop. It had become a comfortable routine, especially now that her father was in much better health.

Afterwards, Miles and her father headed back to work as usual. Abigail fetched the pile of dresses she needed to finish, Pat helping her to gather all her sewing supplies before sitting herself down on the comfy chair in the front of the shop to get stuck in. Usually, she'd be flitting about all over the place and working through the back where she had plenty of space but she was six months gone and being pregnant was no easy feat.

Tiredness overcame her easily and it was getting

harder and harder to move about. *It's worth it,* she thought, in *just three months I'll be meeting our little one.* Sometimes when she had a moment to herself, she lost herself in wonderment, thinking about how lucky she was to finally marry the man of her dreams and begin a family of their own. She could hardly wait for the baby to arrive.

Your mother would be so proud of you, her father had said, his eyes glistening with pride, on the day of their wedding. She'd created and stitched her own dress, having spent weeks putting it together and painstakingly attaching the beads and ribbon. Everyone had gushed about how beautiful it was, wanting to know where she had got it. When she admitted that she'd sewn it herself, she became inundated with requests to commission her to make dresses, or with impressed admirers insisting that she open her own dressmakers' shop.

Auntie Pat overheard, agreeing enthusiastically and a matter of weeks later Walter's Dress Shop was opening its doors to the public.

Miles had been delighted with the idea, encouraging her all the way through. He'd got to work on reorganising the back shed attached to the townhouse which was empty and disused. Pretty soon it went from dark and dusty to a bright and beautifully decorated space, laid out perfectly so that the front part made up the shop entrance and then behind the curtain lay the workshop and storage area.

"Why, this is wonderful!" Abigail had exclaimed when Miles finally let her in to have a look. She wasn't allowed to peek at it until it was done, as Miles wanted to surprise her.

"Where did you learn to do all this?" She couldn't get over how different the place looked and as a merchant's son she figured that learning carpentry wasn't something he would have encountered, let alone mastered to this degree.

"I spent a lot of time repairing and fixing up the shop and house for father when I was growing up," Miles explained. "He only ever believed in one thing and that was hard work."

Jerome hadn't been invited to the wedding but after some encouragement from Abigail, Miles had written to his father to inform him that Abigail and he were married. Some months later Miles received a response. It was short and to the point; just the words *'Congratulations. Hope you survive it.'*

Miles crumpled it up and threw it in the fire in disgust, explaining to Abigail his father's views on marriage. "To him, love does not exist. Marriage is merely a way of getting what he wants and then when it sours, it's a hindrance and waste of time." He'd also never forgiven his father for trying to get him out of the picture so he could force Abigail into marrying him instead. It was a shame that Jerome couldn't just be happy for his only son but Abigail hardly wanted to have anything to do with him.

The bell above the door sounded, bringing her out of her reverie and back to the present as she stood to greet Mrs Lowe, a very well-to-do neighbour who kept her facial expression a blank mask of disdain at all times.

Abigail was forever in fear of disappointing or offending her without intending to but despite her frosty nature, Mrs Lowe kept returning to the shop for dresses both new and to help give old and worn gowns a new lease of life.

Abigail figured she must be doing something right if

Mrs Lowe of all people was satisfied with her. After she left, she had only two more ladies to see before she'd be done for the day.

Miles was nearing the end of his studies, getting more and more responsibilities in the solicitor's office. Garth was working in Miles's office as an accountant, earning double the amount of money he was getting at the Walter's Greengrocer.

Since Abigail's seamstress shop opened up, she'd gained more customers than she could hardly keep up with. So much so that she'd had to turn down commissions which only made people offer her more money. Word had got around that Abigail was the best seamstress they'd ever seen and she had endless requests for unique outfits. Between them, they were better off than Abigail had ever imagined.

It was one month before the baby was born that they moved into their very own cottage. Living in the townhouse with Auntie Pat and her father had been lovely but if they were to be starting a family of their own, they needed their own home. A brand-new space to begin this new journey together.

Between them, they'd saved up enough money to do

up the old cottage just down the street from the townhouse. Miles would go down in the evenings after work and his studies to help fix up the house. Slowly but surely it turned from something musty and old to a thing of beauty.

"Just like everything you touch," Abigail had said teasingly.

"Well, of course, with an inspiration like you," he had said in reply, fixing her with one of those smiles that made her feel like the only woman in the world.

Their first night in the cottage was celebrated with a lavish meal cooked on their new stove. Her father and Auntie Pat arrived laden with food, wine and a gift to welcome them into their new home.

"Welcome! Come in, come in!" Abigail opened the door wide, beaming at them. She was thrilled to be welcoming the first guests into their new home. It was the kind of experience she'd dreamed about all those years ago when they lived in the East London hovel. It was something they'd never wanted to do in that small one-roomed home that reeked of damp and sewage from the street outside.

"Oh, my dear, you'd better get off your feet," Pat

clucked at her as she came in, taking in the sight of Abigail in her apron. Her sleeves rolled up as she was in the midst of preparing an apple crumble for pudding.

No matter how much Abigail protested, Pat was giving her no choice in the matter, pulling out a chair in the kitchen, piling up the cushions and ushering her to sit down with her feet up. Pat bustled around the kitchen, taking over making the apple crumble, the sharp tangy scent mingling with the soothing sweetness of the sugar and spices.

Abigail had to admit, it was a relief to take a rest. Her feet were aching and her back was starting to struggle. She gratefully accepted the drink of water Pat placed in front of her, it was like she instinctively knew what Abigail needed. She was feeling more and more like the mother she'd never had.

As they sat down to eat, Miles made sure she sat back and relaxed, dishing out the slices of freshly roasted meat and spoonsful of their home-grown vegetables, roast potatoes and gravy on the side. Her father poured out generous helpings of wine which Pat eagerly distributed around the table.

When their plates were empty and nobody could possibly swallow another mouthful, Garth straightened his walking stick and pushed himself up to standing.

"Well, here's to Abigail and Miles and your first night in your new home," he said raising a glass. They all held up theirs along with him, saying *'cheers.'*

"Now, we have our own special announcement to make," he continued, turning to speak in Abigail's direction. "You and Miles are about to begin your own family and, well, Pat and I are embarking on one of our own. Or rather expanding the one that we have. It was certainly a surprise to both of us but a happy one all the same."

"Wait, so... I'm going to be a big sister?" Abigail exclaimed, completely taken by surprise as what he was saying sunk in.

"Yes, yes you are," Garth said, beaming at Pat as the pair of them cosied up to each other.

Abigail felt a warm glow of happiness as she watched them. For as long as she could remember, she'd never seen her father truly happy. All those years of struggle were filled with illness and the pain of losing Abigail's mother. Now it was like he'd come to life again since Pat and he were married. A baby was certainly something to celebrate.

Auntie Pat had distanced herself from Jerome Walter, her only brother, and had been set to marry Ronald Bennett many years ago. He was a solider and rather high up in the ranks and had provided for her and their family-to-be before shipping off to war. Pat had been pregnant with their child but she lost it after hearing the news that Ronald had been killed in battle. She managed to survive the miscarriage, the only silver lining being that her late fiancée' had left her the house and all his assets.

She'd told Abigail about how painful it had been living in the house all by herself, surrounded by nothing but memories and moments that never came to pass. She then closed up the house for the summer months to go and spend time with her parents, hoping that time away in the fresh air would heal her mind. She hadn't been able to face going back until Miles came to her needing her help.

"You're like a daughter to me, Abigail," Pat said. "I'm

overjoyed at being able to fill this house with my new family. It's given the place a whole new lease of life."

"Well, congratulations are certainly in order," Miles announced as he stood up and raised his glass to the happy couple.

"Oh yes, congratulations!" Abigail agreed, smiling at the infectious feeling of joy in the air.

"To family," Pat agreed, raising her own glass. They all followed suit and repeated her words back to her before taking the obligatory sip of wine after a toast.

Soon, the baby arrived. It was a little girl just like Abigail had longed for. They named her Marie and she was the light of their little family. Miles insisted that she looked just like Abigail, with big pretty eyes and beautiful blonde curls.

Garth was overjoyed at the sight of his granddaughter. "She has your mother's looks," he commented wistfully as he held her in his arms, gazing down into her face with wonder.

"Which means she'll be a beautiful princess when she grows up," Abigail said fondly.

"Just like her mother," Garth said, smiling up at her.

Seven months later Miles was a fully qualified solicitor and baby Jamie was born; Abigail's brother and playmate to Marie. Miles had his own solicitor's office, Abigail opened a bigger shop next door, hiring other seamstresses to help and helping to train up new girls. She had enough help that she could work less, spending plenty of time with her daughter, husband and helping Auntie Pat with baby Jamie.

It was the life she and Miles had always wanted and she couldn't be happier.

I hope you enjoyed this first book of mine. I have 3 more currently undergoing editing. To find out when they will be available join my newsletter at http://eepurl.com/dOVZDb

READ on for a preview of my next book.

THE ORPHANS COURAGE PREVIEW

*V*aleria Collins squinted as the dull, grey light filtered through the filthy window. She stifled a yawn and tried to wake to another dreary morning of cold and spitting rain. It was typical of London at this time of year.

Her first thought was surprise that Miss June, the woman who ran the orphanage, hadn't made them scrub the cracked glass, with vinegar and newspaper, for at least a week. Her second was one of cold and discomfort. The wind howled through the gaps in the window and ran over her shoulder. Trying to pull the thin, dirty blanket up, she wished that Caroline would stop kneeing her in the back.

A shiver ran through her, and she huddled under the thin blanket, inching closer to her pallet mates. Despite the fact that Caroline slept in a tight ball, at least she was warm. Lucy snuggled closer to Valeria in her sleep, snuffling in the little girl way that she had even though she was nearly eight. To one side, Nora, her best friend, looked cold and small. Her thin body shook and Valeria moved closer to her, inching the blanket over her shoulder.

Then she cuddled back down and savoured the last few minutes of rest before they were all roused from sleep. Valeria tried not to think about the day ahead of her, which would include the same never-ending drudgery that it always did. The girls would start with whatever chores Miss Jane decided to assign them for that day. Scrubbing and cleaning the house, cooking the water-thin gruel, or sweeping out the hearth were all possibilities, and she was never sure which one she dreaded the most.

Then after a bit of food, the girls would start the mending that Miss June took in so that she could earn some extra money. Valeria flexed her fingers, trying not to feel bitter about the fact that her hands always ached as did her eyes from squinting in the dim light that their paltry candles offered.

With a sigh, Valeria lifted herself off the pallet, trying not to disturb the other girls. Pulling on her tattered dress, she wondered how she would ever get adopted when she looked like a dirty waif you would find on the street. She would try to clean herself up before anyone else awoke. Sweeping her brown hair back into the ribbon she kept in her apron pocket, she decided to go outside.

Everything squeaked and creaked as she crept down the hallway to the stairs that would lead her to the kitchen. There she might be able to sneak the bucket out to the pump in the back. She knew that if Miss June caught her, she would be punished; taking the bucket to the pump was not something she was allowed to do just for herself. None of the girls were allowed to leave the building without permission. She knew that she would probably be emptying the chamber pots for the next month if she was caught. Still, she couldn't bear to go through another day so dirty and dishevelled and they only got water to wash on a Wednesday which was three days away.

As she made it to the bottom step, she heard the tell-tale clicks of low-heeled boots coming down the hallway. There was no mistaking the sound as that of Miss June.

Panic flashed through Valeria, making her heart beat so fast that it thrummed in her ears. She could not be caught. Looking around quickly, she decided to take her chances in the hall closet.

Ducking behind the door, Valeria held her breath as Miss June walked by. Only then did she realize that there was a second set of footsteps. She wondered who would be walking with Miss June this early in the morning.

"I have sent out a notice to some of our... wealthier supporters," Miss June was saying. The pair had stopped in front of the closet, so Miss June's voice echoed through the small entryway.

"What for?" Valeria recognized the voice as that of Mrs. Mulligan, the housekeeper for the wealthy widow who lived next door to the orphanage. What was she doing here this early?

Miss June sighed heavily. "We need to get some of the older orphans out of here. There have been many inquiries for placements here, so many people going to the poor house, but we do not have enough room. Not that it will stop me, but I don't think I can stand too many more brats under this roof and the older girls are more trouble. They eat more too."

"So, how many people will be coming?" Mrs. Mulligan asked.

"I'm not sure, but as many as we can get," Miss June said. "You need to try to get that employer of yours over here. The old bat would be a good benefactor. With her support, I wouldn't have to take in so much work."

Valeria tried to understand every word. The main thing that she was hearing was that she had a chance today to get adopted. It was the thing that she longed for more than anything in the world. It made her want to get cleaned up all the more. How she wished Miss June would move on. Holding her breath, she tried to imagine what it would be like to have a real home. There would be food every day and maybe even meat on a Sunday. It was a dream that put a smile on her face. This time it would be her.

After what seemed like an eternity, the two women

were on their way disappearing to another part of the building.

Valeria eased out of her hiding place, and as she stood debating whether or not now was the right time to try to get out to the pump, she heard some of the other orphans coming down the stairs. Her spirits fell. Now wasn't the right time, but she had to get cleaned up before the prospective adoptive parents came.

As Valeria headed to the kitchen area to start what she hoped would be her chores for the day—cooking was the least despicable task she could think of—she bumped right into Nora, her closest friend in the orphanage.

"Oh, Nora, sorry!" Valeria cried. "I guess I was just preoccupied."

"Is something bothering you?" Nora asked, tilting her head to one side so that her thin blond hair spilled over her shoulder.

Valeria chewed on her lower lip, and then lowering her voice, said, "I heard Miss June say that a lot of people are coming today for adoptions."

"Oh," Nora said. "That's nice."

Valeria felt the rising irritation in her chest. Nora was two years younger than she was, and sometimes in moments like this, Valeria could tell that the age gap made the younger girl slightly naive.

"I really want to get adopted," Valeria said.

Nora nodded. "I know you do, me too."

"I've been studying so hard," she said. "I found a book of poetry hidden behind the drawers in one of the attic rooms and I have been practicing my reading. And I don't know if you noticed or not, but I've been practicing my manners as well."

"You'll get adopted one day," Nora said encouragingly.

Valeria had to admire the younger girl's optimism in the face of the bleakness that surrounded them on a daily basis.

"You will too," Valeria said impulsively. She wasn't sure she believed the words, but she wanted to. "Just think what it will be like when we get out of here and have a real family."

"Warm beds and full bellies," Nora said, her eyes glazing over at the thought."

"Someone who actually cares about what happens to us." Valeria was smiling as the fantasy felt so tantalizingly close.

"No one is ever going to care what happens to you."

The snooty voice broke through the sweetness of the daydream. Valeria turned to scowl at Sophie Walsh, her arch enemy in the orphanage. Sometimes she wanted to slap the freckles off the other girl's smug face.

"Any of us could get adopted today," Nora piped up.

"I wasn't talking to you," Sophie snapped at Nora, propping her hand on her hip. She turned back to Valeria. "You are practically an old maid. You will be sent to the workhouse before any person is dumb enough to take a chance on you."

Valeria felt a panic inside, not the workhouse, she believed it was even worse than here and she wouldn't go there... ever. "I am going to get adopted," Valeria said with a ferocity that made the other girls' eyes widen slightly.

Sophie recovered quickly, the smirk returning to her face. "Please, you've never been anyone's first choice. You haven't even been anyone's second choice. You're just ugly and pathetic."

"You haven't been anyone's first choice either," Valeria retorted fighting down the sting that the other girl's words caused inside. "Or else you wouldn't be here."

"As a matter of fact, I've been plenty of people's second choice," Sophie said.

Before Valeria could say anything else, however, the tell-tale clicking of boots came back down the hall.

Miss June grabbed Valeria by the elbow and moved her to one side. She glared between the three girls.

"Stop this bickering, all of you. We'll not have any of that today," Miss June yelled as her face melted into a glower. "All three of you will scrub floors until I can see myself in them. Otherwise, you won't get your soup tonight."

As the three of them trudged silently away, Valeria vowed that she would do her chores and then clean up so that she would find the perfect people to adopt her.

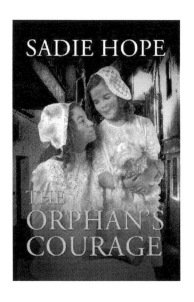

THE ORPHANS COURAGE will be available soon join my newsletter to find out when.

Sadie Hope was born in Preston, Lancashire, where she worked in a textile factory for many years. Married with two grown children, she would spend her nights writing stories about life in Victorian times. She loved to read all the books of this era and often found herself daydreaming of characters that would pop into her head.

She hopes you enjoy these stories for she has many more to share with you.

You can find Sadie:

On Facebook

or

Follow her on Amazon search Sadie Hope

March 20 19

Printed in Great Britain
by Amazon